20.99

THE SILVER-MINE SPOOK

A fabled silver-mine leads a dying prospector and his fiery niece to the peaceful Colorado town of Silver Bluff — but things don't remain peaceful for long. Stalked by a criminal who will stop at nothing to get his hands on untold wealth, they enlist the help of Marshal Jim Morgan, a man running from his past. The three soon find themselves caught in a web of deceit, tangled motives and the schemes of a gypsy fortune-teller whose cards promise death . . .

LANCE HOWARD

THE SILVER-MINE SPOOK

Complete and Unabridged

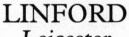

LINFORD
Leicester

First published in Great Britain in 2003 by
Robert Hale Limited
London

First Linford Edition
published 2004
by arrangement with
Robert Hale Limited
London

British Library CIP Data

Howard, Lance
    The silver-mine spook.—Large print ed.—
Linford western library
1. Western stories
2. Large type books
I. Title
823.9′14 [F]

ISBN 1–84395–300–5

Published by
F. A. Thorpe (Publishing)
Anstey, Leicestershire

Set by Words & Graphics Ltd.
Anstey, Leicestershire
Printed and bound in Great Britain by
T. J. International Ltd., Padstow, Cornwall

This book is printed on acid-free paper

For Tannenbaum

1

'What the hell's this town doin' here, Grace?' Phidias Crowly spat in disgust and ran a buckskin-covered forearm across his mouth, wiping away spittle from the sagebrush mustache drooping over his upper lip. Gaze narrowing, disappointment swept across his watery eyes.

'Maybe you just misread the sign?' The young woman beside him sitting on the palomino frowned a questioning frown then fished a ragged brown parchment from her saddle-bags. Snapping open the document, she sighed and the frown deepened. Crowly could tell she was having doubts as to his sanity and the ever-growing prospect that he had led her on a thousand-mile, silver-coated wild-goose chase.

The bay beneath him nickered and Crowly cast his niece a you're-not-too-old-to-turn-over-my-knee look.

She ignored him, shifting in her saddle and snapping the map open again after a gust flipped it closed. The palomino's ears twitched and the animal blew a snort of discontent.

'Keep your shoes on, you ornery nag.' She patted the palomino's neck.

'You best be talkin' to that jugheaded horse of yourn.' Phidias nudged his head at the animal. The horse, Ruthie, was given to fits of the 'I won'ts' — I won't budge another inch if you don't have anything better to do than sit there snapping paper — and inclined to moments of sheer snipe-headedness where she took a notion to buck a body straight out of the saddle without the slightest provocation then flash a damned-as-you-please horse grin after doing it.

Grace surveyed the old man with a combustible mix of exasperation and saddle fatigue. 'Least Ruthie knows which ways we're s'posed to go . . . '

Crowly's saddle creaked as he sat straight up. With another gust the scent of sweat and old tobacco wafted up from his person, blending with the musky-sweet aroma of spruce and flowers covering the low hills to the left side of the trail. 'When she goes at all — hell, I've been prospectin' near to thirty years; reckon I damn well know how to read sign by now.'

'You reckon, huh? When was your last strike again?' Irritation sharpened her tone.

A prickle of annoyance burrowed under his own hide as he peered at his niece. Hell, the way her trousers and bibshirt hid her God-given feminine attributes, it was damn hard to figure out she wasn't a nephew. She'd yanked her fawn-colored hair into a bun tight enough to give her green eyes a slant and jammed it up under her Stetson. Grime smudged her face and neither had taken a bath in a spell. How the hell did she ever expect to attract a husband that way?

He shook his head. Grace wasn't the type of filly who needed a man takin' care of her. She was too damn much like her no-good uncle and that saddened him — and made this mission all the more crucial. He saw it as his last chance to make certain she amounted to more than he ever was, a feeble-minded old coot chasing windmills all his life.

With the hurt reflected in Crowly's cloudy blue eyes Grace's face softened and her shoulders slumped. 'Hell, Phid, I reckon I know never finding that big strike eats your belly out sideways and you got everything ridin' on this one. I shouldn't have thrown it in your face.'

A sigh escaped his lips. 'Maybe you got a right to, but I swear I read that map right. This here's where it's s'posed to be, least in this area.'

'Pfft, this here map's fifteen years old. Lots of things change in that amount of time, assuming they was ever the way they was s'posed to be in the first place.'

Phidias's gaze waxed distant. 'Jacob swore with his dyin' breath this strike of silver had veins as pure as prairie snow, more than any man could ever want for.'

'Then why didn't he mine it himself? All you got is this piece of paper and a claim that may or may not be real.'

'Hell, it's real enough . . . ' He twisted in the saddle and pointed at a rock formation behind them, nearly a mile down the trail. The formation resembled a face with a jutting angular nose. 'Big Nose Injun, like it says on that there map. Says to ride on twenty minutes at a horse walk, straight as the arrow flies.'

'Map says a lot of things and all of it in some crazy man's code only you got a notion how to translate. The damn mine probably never existed in the first place.'

Crowly's face set in deeper lines and cold sweat trickled down his sides, despite the warmth of the late-spring day. 'It exists . . . ' He struggled to make his voice sound more confident than he felt. 'It has to. I got too much ridin' on this.'

'Then why's that town sittin' there? Map don't say nothin' about a town. 'Sides, a body would take the notion that if a silver-mine existed someone in that town would have discovered it by now.'

He couldn't rightly argue with her logic. Hell, the town sat there plain as could be, not more than a half-mile down the embankment atop which they sat. No mirage, it was a ramshackle affair of mismatched buildings and a wide main street. He spotted townsfolk roaming the boardwalks, but no silver-mine, least as far as he could see. The doubt embedding itself into his soul grew more powerful.

Grace folded the map and stuffed it back into her saddle-bags. She gazed at him, as if questioning their next move.

'What the hell you lookin' at me that way fer?' was all he could think of saying and she let out a sarcastic *pfft*.

'We best ride in 'fore Ruthie takes a notion she don't want to go no further.' She winked, but he could see weariness

6

simmering behind her eyes.

He nodded. 'Reckon we best — '

A blast cut off his words and he jolted. Lead plowed into the ground inches from Ruthie's left front hoof and the palomino suddenly danced a two-step. Grace, taken by surprise, nearly lost her grip on the reins. She struggled to hold on as the horse neighed in fright and bolted down the embankment.

Phidias bellowed a curse as his own horse jigged about. He wondered where the shot had come from and why, but got little time to think on it. Heeling his horse into motion, he followed Grace down the grade, in case whoever fired decided to trigger a second round.

The horse navigated the slope in lunges and hops and each time its hoofs slammed into the ground a shock of pain shuddered through his bones. A sudden spiking tightness clamped across his chest and he winced, letting out a small groan.

Christ, please, not now . . .

Ahead, Grace was fighting to bring Ruthie to a stop. He angled towards his niece, pulling up beside her just as the young woman coaxed the palomino to relative calm.

She cast him a sour glance. 'Was someone shootin' at us?' The flutter in her voice betrayed the air of toughness she sought to present.

A nervous laugh cascaded from his lips. 'Now that's a plumb asinine question, ain't it?'

'Didn't strike me as such, you old bastard.' She was lying; he could see a scarlet flush of embarrassment blooming on her cheeks.

'Well, hell's bells, what'd you think it was — a mountain cat poppin' his knuckles?'

She twisted her lips into a sneer. 'Reckon you got a point, but I still say it was a good question.' Her eyes challenged him to say different.

He sighed. 'Have it your way. We got bigger things to worry about, such as who was shootin' and why.'

'Best I not find out . . . ' She laid a slim hand on the gun strapped to her right hip. A twinge of worry plucked at Phidias's belly. Grace was as hot-headed as a prairie dog yanked out of his hole by the tail and she knew how to use that piece better than most men.

'We best see if this here town has itself a marshal instead of sittin' on our britches makin' ourselves a target.' He glanced backwards at the rise, but glimpsed nothing suspicious, no glint of sunlight on gunmetal, no pursuing shooter.

Grace forced a smile. 'Hell, that's the first sensible thing you said since we left Texas.'

He frowned, a growing suspicion warning him that while they hadn't found the silver-mine they might have stumbled across something worse. 'Second thought, maybe we best just turn around and go home . . . '

'*What?*' Her eyes darkened like a blue norther sweeping over the Plains. 'We come all this way to find ourselves a silver-mine and now you just take a

9

notion to turn back with your tail between your legs on account of some hunter bein' careless with his rifle?'

He saw in her eyes she didn't believe it was really any accident but almost laughed at the contrariness of her words. Just a few minutes ago she had practically told him they were on a fool's errand and now she wanted to see it through. He knew if he confronted her on the point she'd tell him that was what she had said all along.

'Reckon you're right . . . ' he mumbled, casting another glance behind them. Still no sign of anyone or anything.

'Hell, I'm always right!' She grinned.

'So you delight in tellin' me.' Gigging his horse into a trot towards the town, he heard Grace mutter an obscenity behind him.

★   ★   ★

'What in the goddamn hell do you think you're doin'?' snapped Orville

10

Wilkins from atop his horse after ruining Reb Parker's aim by slapping the Winchester barrel sideways as the hardcase had pulled the trigger.

Reb, hard face twisting with barely concealed fury, drilled Orville with a surly narrowing of his eyes. 'We don't goddamn need 'em anymore. Cain't have no loose ends.'

Orville let out a grunt and plucked his derby from his head. He brushed dust off his suit coat, making sure the flap fell away from the Smith & Wesson in its holster and the Bowie knife sheathed at his hip. Taking a slow shuddering breath, he ran a hand over his pomaded hair, which was parted in the middle. A gaunt man with a thin waxed mustache, he had a high forehead and eyes that somehow brought to mind an owl.

A few feet away, a third man sat on a horse, watching the proceedings, bemused interest playing on his hard face. A large man, well over six feet in height, with stringy black hair and a tangled beard. The man was a mute, capable only of grunting and uttering strangled sounds. An Apache had carved out his tongue years back.

Orville's gray eyes glittered with viciousness as they shifted back to Reb Parker. Struggling to keep his voice level, he let just enough rage bleed through to inform Reb in no uncertain terms just who led the operation. 'Are you plumb loco? We ain't got a clue how to read that map. Only the old man does.'

Reb gazed down the rise at the now empty trail, crimson spreading across his cheeks. With a grunt, he jammed the Winchester into a saddleboot. 'Hell, we've arrived, ain't we? He led us where we're goin'. Lettin' him and that spitfire gal go on breathin's the part that's plumb loco.'

Orville's laugh rang with a heavy dose of mockery. 'You see a goddamn silver-mine anywhere around?'

Reb flinched, reluctantly shook his head.

'That's a town, you stupid sonofa-bitch, not a silver-mine, case you can't tell the difference. We ain't found that mine yet and that old man's the only one with a notion how to read that map. I couldn't make heads nor tails out of it. Didn't find no one else who could, neither. Damn thing is real, though, and it could be the biggest silver strike the West has ever seen, bigger than Leadville.'

Reb's expression darkened. 'Then you sure as hell don't want them two around sharin' in it.'

Reb was an idiot, in Orville's estimation, more like to think with his pecker than what few brains the Lord had seen fit to present him with. However, he was good with a gun and ruthless; the time would come when that was needed. But not yet. In truth, Orville didn't care a lick whether Reb buried the old man. Crowly was headed for bootyard on his own, by the looks of things. Still, when it came to Grace, a twinge of regret twisted in his belly. She fixed up right pretty and, growing up, Orville had always entertained the notion she would be hell in the hay. He aimed to test that theory before Reb killed her. Course, he knew she would never take to him, not as a wife or anything like that. She was too wild, unbreakable, and had kicked the living daylights out of his southern parts one time when they were young'ns after he snuck up on her bathin' in a river and tried to put his hands on her charms. He would have the last word on that account, though, and he damn well wouldn't let Reb ruin it for him.

As he focused back on the hardcase, Parker seemed to shrink under his reproachful gaze. Orville learned long ago when a fella such as himself didn't have brawn he needed another edge, a more deadly edge. What he didn't get through muscle he got through intimidation and domination. Every man had a weakness, one that could be exploited, and Reb Parker proved no exception.

Reb Parker had a sister. The hardcase was a sonofabitch in every sense of the word but when it came to his one remaining kin he was downright protective — and vulnerable. Orville made certain that vulnerability was utilized to the fullest, ensuring Reb didn't take the notion to turn his fast gun on his employer. Parker's sister resided in a home for the infirmed, likely dyin' of whatever disease had made her legs useless as tits on a bull. Orville owned that home — one of the many assets he stood to lose soon if he didn't acquire the large influx of capital this silver strike would provide — and Reb knew it. Orville had graciously offered to provide Parker's sister with the best of care for life — for a price, the price of having an enforcer along on this excursion in case things didn't go the way Orville planned. Of course, Orville would back-shoot Reb the moment he outlived his usefulness. He would make sure to have that sister thrown out of the home, too. She was just a waste of resources and paying space, way he saw it, the no-good cripple.

Orville laughed to himself at the prospect. He had planned everything so well, right from the moment the old man came to him in trust and showed him that map until now — until a goddamned town showed up instead of a silver-mine. A measure of uneasiness crept over him. What if there were no mine? That damned old man had been wrong many times before; what said he would be right now?

Christ on a crutch, he had to be right or Orville would face ruin — and worse. But desperation sure as hell didn't turn fool's gold into ingots.

Letting out a low curse, he shook off the doubt and concentrated on Reb. 'You go off half-cocked again and you'll be sportin' a third peeper in your forehead. I make myself clear?'

Reb shifted in the saddle, looked at the ground, then back to Orville, plainly irked. 'Reckon I got it straight . . . ' Something in the man's dull eyes told

16

Orville Reb wanted nothing more than to put a bullet in him right here and now and even the notion of his sister was barely holding him back.

'We best watch our backs, now. They'll likely go straight to the marshal and tell him what happened.'

Reb shrugged. 'So? They got no notion who did it and the old man don't know we're here. Marshal will write it off as an accident.'

Orville considered that. Parker was right. The lawdog could do little at this point and likely wouldn't put much effort into tracking down a stray shot. 'We best make sure it stays that way and keep watch on that old man till he locates the mine.'

Reb let out a dubious laugh. 'If there is one.'

Rage welled in Orville, flooding his veins and making him react before he could stop himself. He snatched his Smith & Wesson from its holster and jerked it upward in a crisp arc. He was just close enough to Parker to nail the hardcase clean on the point of the jaw. The blow sounded with a bone-shattering *clack* and Reb's eyes rolled up. The hardcase fell sideways out of the saddle and hit the ground hard. Orville feared for a moment the blow had killed the bastard but Reb groaned and pushed himself up on an elbow. The hardcase dragged the back of his hand, across which snaked a long scar, over his bloody lip, which he'd bitten into when the blow snapped his teeth together.

He spat a stream of blood and saliva. 'Jesus, you bastard . . . ' He glared at Orville, who swung the Smith & Wesson to aim on the hardcase's forehead.

Reb's glare iced over and Orville wondered for a moment whether the man would lose all control and thoughts of his kin and try for his gun. He almost hoped that would happen. A fever for blood burned in his veins. Sometimes killin' was just plain enjoyable.

Resignation pushed the anger from

the hardcase's face and he staggered to his feet. After slapping pine needles from his clothing, he hoisted himself back on to his mount. Orville smiled the smile of a cottonmouth and holstered his gun.

'You best never take the notion to mock me again, Parker. You want that sister of yours taken care of you'll do what I say without question.'

Parker remained silent, the only sign he heard a muscle stuttering beside his eye.

2

What the hell am I doin' in a town like Silver Bluff anyway?

Marshal Jim Morgan must have asked himself that question a thousand times since he'd pinned on the tin star six months ago. The answer always came back the same: wallowing in self-pity, though he'd be damned if the knowledge made a lick of difference.

He was still here, wasn't he? Playing lawdog to a town as isolated and peaceful as any Colorado had ever given rise to. Hell, last death had been that of the former marshal and that proved to be an accident. Nothing untoward occurred in Silver Bluff and nothing the least bit exciting ever happened in his sad excuse for a life.

At least since *she* had left . . .

You best face the fact she ain't never gonna change her mind and want you back, Morgan. Not in this lifetime.

For the past six months he had clung to that slim hope, but, hell, when he looked at things from her perspective he was forced to admit maybe she wasn't entirely at fault. He would never be anything more than what he was, an underpaid lawdog; he was lucky to pull down thirty-five greenbacks a month, plus board in the form of a room above the office. That was no sum upon which to raise a family, let alone attend to the tastes of a woman the likes of the Lady Wescott, as she was wont to call herself. Lady Cynthia Wescott. No, he could never support a woman with such refined and extravagant tastes in the style to which she was accustomed, so it should have come as no surprise when she presented him with his walking papers the instant a better and more lucrative offer came along.

But it still hurt like hell.

Staring out through the grime-coated office window, his gaze scuttled along the wide main street. Specters of steam curled from the ground, which was drying after a midnight rain had pounded it to muck; horses' hoofs and wagon wheels had done the throughway a disservice. Townsfolk shuffled mechanically along the boardwalk, oblivious to the miserable longings of its practically superfluous lawdog and just about everything else but their workaday world. Like ants more than not. Life went on. Drearily so.

The sun dipped just past the noon point; fool's gold sparkled from water-troughs and glinted off windows. Everything appeared peaceful, way it always did. Banal. Humdrum.

Christ, what's wrong with you, Morgan? Ain't anything worthwhile to you anymore? Why the devil would you even want that woman after the way she betrayed you? You must have sawdust in your head.

He had to stop feeling sorry for himself. He had to quit thinking about what might have been and start looking towards what might be.

What might be?

In Silver Bluff? That was a laugh! The town boasted few ladyfolk of the marrying age, certainly none with whom he could see himself settling. And this job, well, he reckoned that would go nowhere. At best it was a temporary engagement before he moved on again, endeavoring to put as much distance between himself and Austin — and Lady Wescott — as possible. He figured pride had a lot to do with it, maybe foolish pride, but that, at least, was a something she hadn't completely sluiced from his soul that day she left. Not that she hadn't tried right hard.

A sound of hoofs interrupted his reverie and he glanced downstreet to see two riders coming from the direction of the trail. Eyes narrowing, he ran a hand over his three days' worth of stubble, curiosity turning his features. He didn't recognize the old man and the other fella on horseback, though he reckoned he knew by sight just about everybody in Silver Bluff, which, considering the town consisted of a bit north of a hundred people, was no feat, even at a liberal estimate. Watching them draw closer, he grew certain they were headed for his office. Hell, was he reduced to nothing more than the local welcoming committee now?

Christamighty, wait a blasted minute!

Eyes narrowing further, a small whistle escaped his lips. That was no other fella riding next to the old man; it was a woman, though plumb hard to tell from the way she was dressed. Her boyish clothing did its best to conceal all the things that made a woman a hell of a lot more interesting than a fella, but it didn't hide everything. He had to stop himself from staring at the parts of her that bounced with each hoof-fall of her mount.

As they drew near, he moved away from the window. A moment later boots echoed on the board-walk, then the front door rattled open. The old fella stepped in first, doffing his hat and letting loose a cascade of thin white hair. The man's eyes centered on Jim and he detected an odd sense of sadness there, one tinged with something else. Fear? No, that couldn't be right. What would anyone have to fear in Silver Bluff?

'Marshal . . . ' The old man gave a slight nod of greeting. The young woman eased the door shut behind her. Jim's gaze lingered on her. Close up, he could see the flare of her hips — along with the Peacemaker in the gunbelt strapped to her waist — the fullness of her breasts straining against the bib-shirt. As his eyes locked with hers, a shiver went through his southern borders. With those green eyes, he reckoned, she could make a fella turn handsprings — except that from within them came a sudden challenging look as sharp as ice-picks.

'Yeah, I'm a gal, if it's any nevermind to you.' He damn near jolted at the snap in her tone.

'Reckon I can see that, ma'am.' Why

did he suddenly feel like a kid just caught peeking at a naked gal in a river? He moved over to his desk and slung a leg over a corner, folding his hands on his thigh in an effort to look as composed as possible but not doing a very good job of pulling it off.

'Don't call me ma'am.' She glared at him and he nodded.

'Sorry, ah — miss . . . ?'

'You best be.' Her eyes narrowed, eyes that might have been warm and glowing under different circumstances, he caught himself thinking. 'Name's Grace Crowly and this here's my uncle Phid.' She jerked a thumb at the old man, who shifted feet and let out an audible and prolonged sigh.

'Please forgive my niece, Marshal. She ain't used to bein' around folks all that much. Too busy followin' an old man who ain't done his job learnin' her the finer points of life.'

She cast the old man a look that would have chipped rust off a horse-shoe. 'Don't go apologizin' for me, you

26

old bastard. I know how to conduct myself just fine.'

Jim Morgan cleared his throat loud in an effort to head off the war of words he judged was imminent.

'You're new in town?' Morgan nodded to the blue enameled coffee-pot and two tin cups sitting on a small table. 'Offer you some? It's lukewarm, but drinkable.'

The old man declined with a shake of his head and muttered, 'No, but thanks kindly. And to answer your question, we just rode in.'

'And a hell of a welcomin' committee you got here, too, lawdog.' The young woman practically spat the words as she went to the table. She poured herself a cup and took the liquid down in nearly one gulp. Wincing, she looked over at him. 'Hell, you ain't had a woman around in a spell, have you?'

The words stung, reminding him how sorry for himself he had felt only a few minutes before.

'Grace . . . ' The old man's tone was

reproachful and she gave him a withering look, twisting one corner of her mouth while waggling her head. Jim reckoned she might have given Lady Wescott a run for her money when it came to condescending expressions.

'It's OK, Mr Crowly.' Morgan folded his arms, glancing at the woman. 'Reckon she's just tired from being on the trail. Ain't no place for a woman out there.' He put a sarcastic note on it, finding the young woman was getting to him in a way that wasn't entirely unpleasant, though for the life of him he couldn't figure why.

'Hell, you're quite the gentleman, ain't you?' The girl's expression turned snide, tone challenging.

He sighed and shifted his attention back to the old man, knowing a battle with words with Grace Crowly was likely a losing proposition. 'What did she mean by a welcomin' committee? Far as I know we ain't got one. Don't get many visitors here. Fact is, last ones were the gypsies camped near the edge of town and God knows why they stayed on other than the fact most places ain't real keen on having 'em.'

'*I'll* tell you what I meant, lawdog.' She said 'lawdog' with an edge he rightly didn't appreciate. She set the tin cup down with a bang and locked her arms together. He couldn't help noticing the way it enhanced her bosom. 'Some lowly sonofabitch took a shot at us while we were just sittin' on our horses minding our own.'

For the first time he saw a hint of fear cross her eyes. 'You sure about that?'

Her face took on an unhealthy red color. 'Course, I'm sure, you stupid — '

'Grace!' snapped her uncle, tone serious and reprimanding, and this time she clamped her mouth shut, though not without a castigating look for her uncle and snide *pfft* for Jim Morgan.

Hell of a gal, he thought for no reason he could pin-point. Then again, he recollected he'd always loved the one mule that kicked him in the head when he was a young'n. His pa had threatened to shoot it, but Jim had saved its sorry hide and after that he reckoned that mule and him had reached a strange understanding. Grace reminded him of that mule, though he doubted she'd care much for the comparison.

'Fact is,' the old man continued before his niece could get started again, 'someone did take a shot at us, Marshal . . . ?'

'Morgan, Jim Morgan.' He nodded, glancing out through the window at the early afternoon. The street appeared as peaceful as ever and the notion anyone in Silver Bluff would shoot at two newcomers seemed almost ludicrous. 'You sure they were shootin' *at* you?'

'Hell, that bullet damn near took my head off!' Grace's voice carried less of an edge this time.

'They was shootin' at us, no doubt about it,' Crowly put in.

Jim rubbed his chin, a thoughtful expression crossing his face. 'Why, Mr Crowly? What reason would anyone have for shooting at two strangers? Silver Bluff ain't had a lick of trouble in the six months I've been here.'

Crowly looked suddenly uncomfortable and that made Jim wonder if the man were hiding something.

Crowly shrugged. 'Ain't got the faintest, but if that lead had been any closer your funeral man would've had hisself new business.'

Jim's eyes narrowed. 'Where'd it happen?'

'Edge of town, right where the trail drops off sharply.'

'And you were just sitting there mindin' your business when a shot came out of nowhere?'

The old man nodded. 'Reckon that says it in a Winchester shell. Came from the right and up, best I could judge. There's a rise to that side of the trail.'

Jim knew the spot. 'You see anyone?'

Crowly shook his head. 'No, not a soul.'

'Maybe it was a hunter in his cups, a stray shot?'

'Wasn't no hunter, Marshal. It was deliberate. I been on this earth long enough to know that much.'

Morgan raised an eyebrow. 'You get shot at a lot, Mr Crowly?'

He offered a thin smile. 'No, reckon this is a first.'

Jim could see no earthly reason why anyone in Silver Bluff would fire at an old man and his niece, but he did hear a hesitancy in the old man's words, as if he were hiding something.

'Why did you come to Silver Bluff, Mr Crowly? I mean, folks normally don't just ride in here. They either stumble across it on their way to somewhere worth visitin' or avoid it completely.'

The old man shifted feet, cast a glance at Grace, who remained tight-lipped. Jim decided he was hiding something all right, but what?

'Reckon we're just the stumblin' kind, Marshal. Just passin' through. Maybe we shouldn't have bothered you with it. Just wanted to let you know, is all.'

'Why did you want to let me know, Mr Crowly? If you were just passin' through, why didn't you keep on passin'?' Morgan knew he was being a bit hard on the old man but he saw more to the story than Crowly was letting on and his lawman instincts were taking over.

'Hell, what a stupid question — ' Grace took a step towards him.

Crowly held up a hand. 'Now, Grace, Marshal's got a right to ask questions.'

'Just want all the facts, ma'am,' he said before he could stop himself and the girl flashed him a cold glare. He ignored it and stood. 'I'll take a look around out there, but that's likely the most I can do. Whoever shot at you's probably long gone by now. If they got no reason for doin' it you likely don't have any more to worry about.'

Crowly nodded. 'Much obliged, but I reckon no one's got cause to harm us.'

'You plannin' on stickin' around town a spell, or resumin' your passin' through?' Jim glanced at Grace as he

33

asked it and found himself half-wishing she was staying. The thought of the donkey kicking him in the head passed through his mind again.

Crowly twisted at the brim of his hat. 'We're plumb tired from our journey and could use a restover, I reckon.'

Jim bet there was more to it, but for the moment couldn't figure what. 'There's a house at the end of town that rents cheap. Only got one room but don't do much business, considering we don't get many visitors. Tell Mrs Philbert I sent you.'

'Much obliged.' The old man gave him a weary look and Jim felt a strange sense of pity for him. Maybe it was because Crowly had to tolerate a gal like Grace or maybe it was something unspoken, an emptiness that seemed a reflection of his own life, the way he might end up, old, itinerant and unfulfilled.

You're drawin' a hell of a conclusion based on little more than a notion, Morgan. Sure you ain't just feelin' sorry for yourself again?

Crowly moved towards the door, Grace following. The old man stopped and looked back at him. 'Marshal, mind if I ask you somethin'?'

'Askin's free, Mr Crowly.' He smiled.

'This town . . . ' The old man ducked his chin towards the street. ' . . . how long has it been here?'

'Reckon fourteen or fifteen years. Legend says it was built by an old prospector who just up and left it a couple years later. Likely it's just a one of them tall tales, though.'

Crowly nodded, an unreadable look in his rheumy eyes, but one that told Jim the old man had just heard something that struck a chord with him. 'You been marshal the whole time?'

Jim shook his head. 'No, like I said I just came in 'bout six months back. Other marshal met with an unfortunate accident.'

'What happened to him?'

'Damn fool was climbing around

35

some rocks at the end of town near where them gypsies got their camp and fell off. Way he hit his head he musta died right away.'

Crowly nodded again, lined face thoughtful. He opened the door and stepped out. Grace cast the marshal a parting glance he couldn't read but some of the chill had drained from her expression.

'Afternoon, Miss Crowly.' He tipped a finger to his forehead. She uttered a sarcastic laugh and banged the door shut behind her.

★ ★ ★

Phidias Crowly halted as he stepped off the board-walk into the street and glanced at Grace, who stopped beside him. 'You didn't have to antagonize him, Grace. It might have made him suspicious.'

She let out a scoffing *pfft*. 'So? Ain't no silver-mine here anyway and, in case you forgot, some fella took a shot at us.

I ain't about to let that p

There she went being

Since he saw little use ar

he changed the su

understand it. Jacob r

starting a town.'

'Hell, he was off his mule. I've ᵗᵒ
you that a hundred times over. All his
big stories . . . never was a lick of
truth to anything he said. Anyone
who found a silver-mine wouldn't just
let it lie.'

'He was a simple man, Grace. He
lived simple and even in the end all he
cared about was gettin' a decent burial.
That's why he gave me the mine. Told
me I was the only one who ever was a
real friend to him. Presented me that
title on his deathbed after I promised to
bury him proper. 'Sides, dyin' men
don't have no reason to lie.'

'Dead men don't tell no tales,
neither, but livin' men sure as hell do,
especially loco ones. Christ ridin' a
donkey, Silver Bluff's a right befittin'
name, if you ask me.'

the hell's that s'posed to

eanin' maybe he got everything
m that mine there was to get and
hat's why he rode off and left this
town. If it was ever there at all it's
probably just a big ol' hole in the
ground now.'

Crowly sighed a weary sigh, her
suspicion pricking at his own doubts.
He recollected Jacob being an eccentric
sort, given to tall tales, though he had
never uttered a word about this mine
until his deathbed. He figured that lent
some credence to the story and he'd
agreed to the old man's dyin' requests
even before he learned of the mine, so
Jacob had no reason to concoct a tale.
Had he simply chosen to believe what
he wanted? Was it just another wind-
mill?

Crowly sighed and shook his head,
worry cinching in his chest. 'Well, we're
here, so we might at least have us a look
around.'

'Ain't much other choice, is there?'

Grace's lips drew tight. He could tell she was in no mood to be reasoned with.

'Except for maybe gettin' shot at again.'

She cocked an eyebrow, face growing serious. 'Who would shoot at us? We ain't got any enemies to tell of and no one knows we're here.'

He shook his head, the same question nagging at own his thoughts. 'Hell if I know. It don't make sense. Like I told you when we started out, I took that map and title to Orville and had him verify them, but he don't know how to read the map and I didn't tell him where I was goin'. 'Sides, Orville wouldn't shoot at us.'

A dark look swept across her eyes. 'Don't be so sure about that. I never did care a lick for his sorry hide. He's got a mean streak, not to mention the rutting habits of a goddamn jackrabbit. Rumor tells, some gals he rode saddle with at the whore-house got themselves black eyes and bruises for their money.'

39

'Hell, those's just rumors. You know how whores talk. Orville's a business-man. He's got a reputation folks want to tear down. He's the one who told me that title was legitimate, remember?'

Grace made a scoffing sound. 'Maybe he wanted it for himself.'

'You're too suspicious of folks, Grace.'

'Give me a reason not to be.'

Phidias grunted, knowing she likely had him there. 'Have it your way.' A note of exasperation hung in his tone.

'I aim to.' She uttered a sharp laugh.

They started walking towards their horses, but Phidias stopped again. A look of shock crossed his face as his gaze settled on a building across the street and for an instant his legs went wobbly. He felt hope shrivel within him. 'El Silverado . . . ' It came out a whisper, his lips barely moving beneath the bushy mustache.

'What're you mumblin' about now?' Grace's tone wielded more than a little irritation.

40

He ducked his chin towards the building. 'That sign . . . name ring a bell?' He couldn't keep the despair out of his voice.

Face darkening, she gave a reluctant nod. 'El Silverado. Same name as on your title.'

He looked at her then back to the sign. *El Silverado*. Burned on to a sign above the batwing doors. A saloon. A saloon with the same name as the title to his silver-mine.

Without further words, he shuffled his way across the street. Grace followed, a disgusted sound coming from her lips. As they reached the batwings, she grabbed his forearm.

'Best you let me go in. You know you can't keep away from whiskey and you know how your mouth starts workin' overtime when you get liquored up. Doc says you ain't s'posed to drink and smoke no more, anyhow.'

'Hell, you'd deny an old man the only pleasures life has to offer?'

'I would if it means you stickin'

41

around extra years. Life's got a hell of a lot more to offer than rotgut and those god-awful cigars you call a pleasure.'

'Does it?' His face pinched and he wondered just what life did have to offer, not for him, because his time was nearly done, but for Grace. She faced the prospect of living out her years the way he had lived his, when she should have been in her prime of life, marryin' and having young'ns, the way a woman was meant to.

'What the hell's that mean?' Anger singed her voice and it was a fight they'd engaged in countless times on the trail. He knew she was using it this time to keep him from entering the saloon. Hell, he couldn't blame her; she had pulled him out of more than a few, droolin' all over himself, pants down around his knees.

'Nothin', it don't mean nothin'.' His voice held a measure of defeat. 'I'm goin' in. You can join me or head on over to that house the marshal told us about and fetch us a room.'

She peered at him, apparently figuring out he had no intention of backing down. 'Awright, I'm goin' with you, then. Someone's gotta keep you sober.'

He nodded and pushed through the batwings. The interior was gloomy, ghosts of dust swirling within the anemic shafts of sunlight that streaked through the grimy windows. The musky combination of cheap whiskey and Durham smoke permeated the air and Crowly savored it like a condemned man tasting a last meal. Other odors, not so savory, blended in: old vomit, stale sawdust and sweat. A long bar ran parallel to the north wall and a handful of men, mostly older gents, sat at tables playing poker. A piano stood against the rear wall, near a door leading to a back area.

At a table near that door sat a woman with black hair that cascaded over bare shoulders. Her dark eyes met his and she smiled the smile of a rattlesnake contemplating a mouse. An off-the-shoulder blouse with puffy armlets and a plunging neckline revealed far more of her ample bosom than he was used to seeing. The sight made his mouth go dry. The ruffles of a peasant skirt peeked out from the side of the table. Large loop earrings hung from her lobes and numerous bracelets of gold, silver and copper ringed her wrists. She clasped a deck of oversized cards, shuffling, cards he didn't recognize but knew had nothing to do with poker or the other games of chance with which he was familiar. A gypsy. He'd heard of them, but had never actually seen one. It wasn't an unpleasant sight. Above her to the right was a sign tacked to the wall that said: *Catriona, Psychic Extraordinaire: Sees all, Knows all, Tells all — for one silver dollar!*

'What the hell you gawkin' at?' Grace's snapping question startled him from his reverie and he looked over to see her pinning a man at the bar with an icy glare. The man grunted and went back to his whiskey. Rough in appearance, with a scar running across the

44

back of his hand, he looked to be a hardcase and Crowly knew he'd better get Grace away from the fella before trouble started. Sometimes she didn't have a lick of sense when it came to who she got riled up.

He grabbed her elbow and herded her to the opposite end of the bar, not far from the gypsy fortune-teller.

'What the devil you doin'? That fella was starin' at us.' Grace's lips drew into a tight line and her cheeks reddened.

'Leave it be, Grace. We don't need trouble and he's got it written all over him.'

She glared but relented, something that didn't happen often enough. They took stools and the saloon-keeper ambled over, a burly man with a wide face and stained teeth.

Crowly plucked a cigar from his pocket and chewed at the end. Grace made a disgusted face but let him have it. Damned if he'd give it up, anyhow. He fished a lucifer from his shirt pocket and puffed the stogie to light. Grace waved off the smoke that drifted her way, cursing.

'What's your poison?' the 'keep asked.

'Whiskey,' Crowly said.

The barman looked at Grace.

'Nothin',' she said with a spiteful lilt.

The 'keep eyed her but she gave him a scowl and he apparently thought better of arguing over it. He grabbed a bottle of whiskey from the hutch behind him and slapped a glass on the counter. After pouring two fingers, he set the bottle down next to the glass.

Crowly nodded and dug in his pocket for a silver dollar, tossed it to the barman.

He wasted no time getting a question off his mind. 'How long's this saloon been here?'

The man shrugged. 'Reckon about fourteen-fifteen years.'

'You always owned it?'

An oddly defensive look crossed the man's face. 'No, fella left it to me.'

'What fella?'

'A prospector fella. Told me it was all mine till someone showed up with the title, but he didn't know how long that'd be. After twelve-thirteen years I figured it wasn't goin' to happen.'

'Mite strange for a fella to do, ain't it?' Crowly tried to make his tone light so the bartender would keep talking.

'Hell, yeah, but if you knew this fella you'd know everything about him was strange. Loco as they come, I figure, but a hell of an *hombre* just the same. Did anything for a friend. And I been right comfortable here until recent-like.'

'Somethin' happen recent-like?' Crowly downed the whiskey. It burned like hell and he fought the urge to cough, then poured himself another. Christ, he knew he was pushing his luck drinkin' and smokin', but couldn't stop himself.

The bartender shrugged. ''Tween you and me, I'm startin' to think things.'

Crowly blinked. 'What kind of things?'

'Well, things like this old place might

have itself a haunt, maybe that old prospector's ghost.'

Grace let out a sharp laugh and the barkeep got an insulted look on his face.

'Grace . . . ' A stern reprimand laced Crowly's tone. Last thing he needed was for the barkeep to go quiet and Grace was like water on a camp-fire.

'If'n you heard the strange clanking goin' on here at night sometimes and that peculiar shuffling noise and creakin' that comes with it, you might start believin' in spooks yourself. Sounds like them noises are comin' right from the walls and floor.'

'Don't say?' Crowly wondered if the man was telling him a tale to stave off any title claim. Had the 'keep gotten suspicious?

'Do say. You'd sing a different tune if'n you heard them. Was thinkin' of sellin' if'n it keeps up.'

'Selling?' Well, that put his theory to rest. If the man was worried about losing his saloon he wouldn't likely have

48

said anything about sellin' it, not to a fella he suspected of owning a title.

'Hell, I ain't gonna stay where it's haunted. Might sell it to that gypsy yonder. She ain't afraid of haunts. She talks to 'em all the time, she tells me.'

Crowly glanced back at the olive-complexioned woman, who gave him the snake smile again. 'How you reckon a gypsy could afford a saloon?'

'She makes plenty tellin' fortunes, I figure, and her fella, he does magic tricks. She makes jewelry, too, outa fine silver. She made me an offer.'

Crowly's brow knotted. 'Why ain't you took it, then?'

The 'keep's face darkened. 'Well, just that this saloon is my life. I got me no real urge to go elsewhere. Silver Bluff is a peaceful little town and I was right happy here till the ghost came a-haunting.'

'Ain't no such critters.' Grace's lips twisted into an expression that said the barkeep was plumb out of his mind for believing in such nonsense.

The 'keep looked insulted again. 'You callin' me a liar, fella?'

Anger flashed across Grace's face. 'In the first place I ain't no fella, you stupid sonofabitch, and in the second I'm callin' — '

'Now, now, Grace.' Crowly clamped a hand on her forearm and squeezed. He looked at the barkeep, whose face had reddened. 'She ain't callin' you anything, my fine man. Just that it ain't everyday you run acrosst a genuine, honest to goodness spook — is it, Grace?' He squeezed tighter, praying she would take the less than subtle hint and shut up before ruining any chance of more information.

She grumbled and turned on her stool to face the barroom, irritation swarming in her eyes.

The 'keep nodded, but appeared unconvinced Grace hadn't been calling into question his honesty. 'Jest be careful who you call what. You stick around you'll be believin' it yourself 'fore long.'

He moved off, muttering. Crowly looked at Grace, who sneered.

'Why you gotta go pissin' on everyone's flowers all the time? You ain't never gonna get a man that way.'

She turned her head away, face pinched. 'Don't need a man. Don't need the trouble.'

'I won't be around forever. I want better than this for you.'

Her voice climbed to a shrill pitch and she locked gazes with him. 'Better than what? Better than doin' what's in the Crowly blood? Ever since my ma and pa died in that fire I ain't wanted to settle any one place and you know it. Settlin' ain't me and neither is tyin' myself down with no fella.'

Crowly's voice lowered with a measure of defeat. 'We've been over this a hundred times. I'll be gone soon — '

'Don't you talk like that, Phid. Just don't you talk like that. I don't want to hear it.'

His face softened, sadness welling within him. 'Best you start facing the facts. I ain't got lots of time and we gotta make plans.'

'Christ ridin' a donkey, I thought that's what we were doin' — makin' plans to find ourselves a silver-mine.'

'Reckon, but they're loco plans, maybe.'

'Damn well looks that way.' She wrapped her arms about herself and he saw the tension rippling through her jaw muscles. She got that look every time he tried to talk to her about his passing and it said she would have no more of it, not now, not ever. She had some unrealistic notion he was going to live forever and though he wished to his Maker that was the God's honest he knew his time was short; denying the fact didn't make it less certain.

He sighed, too weary and a little whiskey-gripped to argue rationally. She would be hit blind-sided when it happened, despite his best efforts. He wondered suddenly if she would cry when he went. He had never seen her shed a tear, not since her ma and pa passed.

Hell, he was getting maudlin and for now that wouldn't do.

'What if I get my fortune told?' he asked suddenly and Grace's mouth dropped open.

'Jesus, Phid, you popped a trace?'

'Just maybe if I showed that gypsy the map she could tell me where the mine is.'

'I can't believe what you're sayin'.' She unfolded her arms and jumped off the stool, jamming her fists into her hips. 'You must be as loco as that 'keep hearing them spooks, or maybe just half-snookered. Ain't no gypsy gonna guide you to that mine. Ain't no mine in the first place. That sidewinder, Jacob, left you a damn saloon, not a mine. El Silverado, don't you get it? It's a goddamn barroom, not a silver strike.' She whirled and stalked towards the batwings.

'Grace, c'mon back — '

She spun and shook her head. 'I stood by you for every false lead and every half-assed whim but I ain't gonna cotton to you stakin' our life on the word of no hornswogglin' gypsy fortune-teller.' She whirled and shoved through the doors. Crowly let her go; he couldn't have stopped her. She would have to cool down first.

He turned on his stool, gulped the rest of the whiskey, then poured another. The liquor shaved off some of the edge, but he had to be careful. He never could handle redeye and for once in his life he had to use his head instead of his heart. He jammed the cigar out on the bartop and buried his face in his hands. He stayed that way for long moments, until a hand gently touched his shoulder. Looking up, he saw the gypsy woman standing behind him, an expression of sympathy in her dark eyes. The sympathy looked as genuine as a whore's smile but right now anything would do.

'Forgive me, old one, but I could not help overhearing.'

Her voice was hard-edged with a practiced sweetness and he nodded.

'Reckon when Grace goes off it's about as subtle as dynamite exploding.'

'You are looking for guidance, no? Catriona can give you such guidance.'

'You're about fifty years too late.' The bitterness in his tone surprised him but the gypsy woman smiled.

'It is never too late, old one. Let Catriona help you.'

It was his turn to smile. 'For a price, like that sign says, if I'm figgerin' right.'

'All things in life come with a price, my friend.' She gave a laugh that had all the ring of cheap glass.

'Reckon you got that right, but what the hell.'

'Come . . . ' Bracelets clinking, she held out her hand and he took it. He had forgotten what it felt like to hold a woman's hand. It unearthed a deep longing for his departed wife, but some of that was the whiskey working. Millie had been gone near twenty years now and that was that.

Catriona led him to a seat at the back table. Lowering herself into her chair, she picked up the cards. They held strange figures he couldn't fathom until she smiled and said: 'The tarot never lies, old one. You are searching, searching for something great, but something that may not be, yes?'

He debated how much to tell her but found the whiskey was loosening his tongue. 'Yeah, reckon I am.'

'Silver, perhaps?' She eyed him, studying his face.

'How the hell . . . ' he started, then wondered if she hadn't overheard Grace and him discussing the mine. Hell, their voices had been loud enough for most of the town to overhear.

'Catriona knows all . . . '

'Yeah, sign says that.' He tried to keep the sarcasm out of his voice, but didn't succeed.

She gave him a scolding smile. 'You must believe. You will keep searching in the wrong place until you do.'

'You got a notion just where the right place would be?'

The snake smile slithered across her

lips and he took the hint.

He fished in a pocket and dug out another silver dollar, placing it on the table. She scooped it up, dropping it between her breasts.

'Tonight, old one. Come tonight and I will contact the spirits. They will tell us where your mine is located.'

'Reckon that'll cost me extra?'

The smile got wider. 'Catriona does not believe in charity.'

'No, don't reckon no one does anymore.' He started to rise.

'You have a woman, old man?'

'No, no she . . . died, twenty years ago. That was my niece you saw.'

'What was her name?'

'Shouldn't you be tellin' me?' The comment brought a disapproving frown from the olive-skinned woman. 'Hell, it was Millie. Dearest woman you ever met.'

'I am certain. Perhaps she will be with us tonight.'

'She's with me always, Miss Catriona, but she don't tell me where things are hidden.'

He moved towards the door, wondering if he had made a mistake trusting the gypsy woman, but hell, even if it were all a fraud it was better than feeling more sorry for himself than he did already.

3

Why would anyone shoot at an old man and his niece?

Jim Morgan sat his horse at the crest of the rise leading on to the trail and gazed at the low hills surrounding Silver Bluff. He could see no reason any of the locals would deliberately target the Crowlys; did that mean they had brought the reason with them?

A niggling suspicion told Jim the old man was concealing something. Did the answer lie down that trail? If it did, was money involved? Motives usually came down to money or passion. Passion appeared off the table but he would have laid bet Crowly didn't have a cent to his name.

Why had Crowly come to Silver Bluff? Was the old man merely passing through, as he claimed, or did he have an ulterior motive for his arrival?

Old silver tales? Certainly, the fella had all the earmarks of a prospector and maybe the rumors of a silver-mine in this area years back had lured him to Silver Bluff. The story wasn't widely known, no El Dorado, and anyone with half a notion in his head took it as a myth. A body had to travel days north to reach the fabled lodes at Leadville. Were camp-fire tales worth killing a man over?

He rubbed his chin. Maybe he was grasping at straws. The old man might simply have been mistaken. The shot could have been an accident. At any rate, it was his duty to check out all probabilities and make certain there wasn't more behind it.

Clucking his tongue, he gigged his horse into motion. Crowly had given him a rough idea of the shot's direction and if Jim recollected right the woodland opened into a clearing above the grade. The roan navigated the rise as if it were a mountain goat.

Reaching the clearing, he stepped

from the saddle and studied the terrain. A chill shivered down his spine as a sense of being watched crept over him. He could little account for the feeling, because he saw no sign of a watcher. Ears pricked, he caught only the sounds of birds twittering, rustles of small animals scampering about, leaves shivering under the breeze. Nothing appeared threatening in the least.

Unable to shake the feeling completely, he moved forward, eyes scanning the ground, noting tiny details such as disturbed twigs and grass coated with irregular dust patterns. A few yards on, he discovered partial hoofprints, at least three horses. Someone had gone to an effort to brush away the tracks but hadn't accomplished the job with any skill. One set led along the clearing's edge and down, as if one of the riders had headed towards town. The other sets ended abruptly at the clearing's edge. It would have taken a master sign-reader to follow them through the woods. A few feet further on he located a cut branch tossed casually aside, its leaves coated with soil. A grim smile pulled at his lips. He knew the branch had been used to wipe out the prints.

Three riders. One shot. Covered tracks. Jim didn't care for where the signs were pointing. Maybe things in Silver Bluff were suddenly a whole lot less mundane than he had thought.

Retracing his steps to where the tracks began, he knelt, eyes roving. A glint caught his attention as sunlight reflected from something nearly buried in a hoof impression. He pried the object from the soil, turning it over in his hand. Whoever shot at Crowly, had used a Winchester, judging by the shell in his palm. With a small grunt of satisfaction, he dropped the casing into his shirt pocket.

Straightening, he peered again at the forest surrounding the clearing, brow furrowed. The shot had been deliberate; Jim felt certain of that now. But the reason still proved elusive. Had Crowly and his niece attracted unwanted attention from itinerant hardcases? Or did it go deeper than that? Was the old man hiding something? That question needed answering, in his estimation, before the shooter decided to make a second attempt on the prospector's life. Or Grace's.

With the thought of the young woman, something in his belly tightened. A strange surge of protectiveness he had no call feeling came over him.

'Christ, Morgan, what are you thinking?' he scolded himself in a mumble. What did that gal matter to him? She had the personality of a rattler and from the way she dressed she did her damnedest to deny she was even a woman.

Fixed up she'd be right pretty . . .

He shook his head, disgusted with himself for a half-formed desire that involved Grace Crowly. That gal was as soft as cactus-needles. Hadn't his less than-stellar entanglement with Lady Wescott saddled him with enough self-pity?

A headache blossoming at the back of his neck, he headed back to his horse, halting a few steps later as a sound caught his ear. Immersed in thought, he wasn't entirely certain he'd heard anything at all, but for a paranoid instant he swore it sounded like a gun hammer ratcheting back. Whirling, his gaze swept the clearing, searching for any hint of danger. Nothing stirred and no further sound came. Even the breeze seemed to still.

He frowned, passing it off as imagination. He went to his mount grabbed the horn and hoisted himself into the saddle. After giving the clearing a last look over, he gigged his horse towards the trail.

* * *

Orville Wilkins didn't breathe until the marshal mounted his horse and rode off. He let the breath out in a relieved shudder and shot a glance at Parker, whose hand held a cocked Smith &

Wesson. Fingers clamped around the hardcase's wrist, Orville released the man as soon as the lawdog was out of sight. Parker gave him a bitter look and holstered the gun. They stood concealed behind a stand of firs, the mute five feet behind them, half hidden behind a large cottonwood.

'You should have let me kill him.' Parker said it through clenched teeth and rubbed his wrist.

'Kill a lawman, you damn fool? We don't need that kind of trouble.'

'We don't need him snoopin' around here, neither.'

Orville nodded, but his blood rushed at the notion of Parker questioning orders again. 'He was just doin' his job. He likely won't be back.'

Reb looked doubtful. 'Hope you're right.'

'What'd you find out at the saloon?'

Parker laughed. 'You was right, that old man can't avoid a bottle. He and that spitfire had themselves a fight loud as could be and the gal stormed out on him. They ain't sure where the mine is, but Crowly had a damned peculiar look on his face when he came into the saloon, like maybe he found somethin' he wasn't expectin'.'

Orville didn't care for the sound of that. Crowly's mine damn well better be here. 'He fetch the marshal after?' Orville looked back to the trail. He had moved the horses to a camp a half-mile west and remained hidden at the outskirts of the clearing until Parker returned from town.

'He must have gone there first. He was too busy with some woman at the saloon and started runnin' at the mouth about the silver-mine. Couldn't rightly hear much of their talk, though.'

'What woman?' Orville's eyebrow cocked.

Reb shrugged. 'Hell, I dunno. Some gypsy fortuneteller. 'Keep told me her fella and her are camped at the other end of town in a couple wagons. Came in 'bout seven months back. She does card-readin' and spirit talks for the locals. 'Keep says she's right on the mark, but then he tells me his saloon's haunted, too, so reckon his deck ain't stacked full.'

Orville blinked. 'Haunted?'

'That's what he said. Crazy sonofabitch, if you ask me.'

Orville cared little for the sudden number of people involved in his once-simple plan to follow the old man and Grace to the mine, then kill them and seize control of the strike. Other factors had been added, all the direct result of Parker's ill-advised shot. He'd make sure a bullet found its way into the hardcase's brain for that blunder.

'They got a séance tonight . . . ' Parker chuckled.

'A what?' Orville's brow knitted.

'Heard the gypsy say she would contact a spirit to guide the old coot to his mine. Bunch of cowflop, you ask me.'

A thoughtful expression came on to Orville's features. 'I'm inclined to agree, but don't it strike you as odd some gypsy would be offerin' such?'

Reb shrugged. 'Hell, no. She's after money, like any of 'em. Haven't seen a gypsy you could trust yet.'

Orville was inclined to agree there, too, but something about the set-up bothered him. He didn't need competition where that silver-mine was concerned.

His demeanor turned serious. 'Maybe you best attend.'

'What the hell you talkin' about?' Parker's eyes narrowed.

'Keep an eye out and see what happens. Don't get too close and for God's sake keep your gun in its holster. I want to know what that gypsy tells the old man. I want to know if she's up to something.'

'She'd tell him anything if he crossed her palm with enough silver.'

'That's exactly what I'm worried about.'

'Don't follow.'

'You don't have to.' Orville smiled but doubts and vague suspicions were starting to work on his nerves. He had come too far to have Crowly louse things up now and he wasn't about to let some small-time swindler take what was rightfully his — the El Silverado mine.

* * *

Catriona dismounted at the far edge of town, just below a bluff of solid rock peppered with piñon and scrub. She glanced at a sprawling patch of brush flush against the bluff's base, then walked towards two large plank-sided wagons angled to her left. In arcing letters the first wagon boasted the words: *Count Junas D'Anguille: Master of Men and Prestidigitator Supreme*; the second wagon carried her name, painted with the same legend as inscribed on the sign in the saloon.

She stumbled on a rock and let out an ungypsy-like curse. Christ, she was sick to death of playing the old country routine, but what choice did she have until they got the saloon into their hands? Plans were progressing but progressing goddamn slowly. And now complications might have presented themselves where she hadn't expected any. She wanted to question the old man further, discover just how he had learned of the silver-mine, but she couldn't appear too curious and arouse his suspicions. Instead, she had fallen back on the same idiotic scare tactics she was employing on the saloon-keeper. She prayed she could misdirect the old bastard before he laid claim to what was rightfully hers. After all, she and Junas had found it, hadn't they? But who would believe a gypsy without a title in her hands? Who would believe a gypsy, period?

If she couldn't misdirect the prospector she would be forced to resort to other means, or rather have Junas do it, the big dumb sonofabitch. He enjoyed strangling almost as much as he enjoyed his silly parlor tricks.

A man stepped from behind a wagon, his heavy black beard jiggling with each step. Dressed in a billowy white shirt smudged with dirt, and heavy brown trousers, his muscles strained at the material and his barrel chest heaved with each breath. A questioning expression laced his wide face. Small dark eyes glittered with cold intent under heavy brows. A bandanna wound about the top of his head and an earring dangled from his left ear. Black boots mapped with scuffs and gouges reached to his knees.

'Why are you back so early, Catriona?' His deep baritone voice carried a timbre that made her want to shudder. 'There is trouble, yes?'

She nodded, a sly look crossing her dark eyes. She strode up to him, grabbing his face and pulling it to her, kissing him deeply. Her tongue wandered into his mouth as she pressed into his arms. Without breaking the kiss, he hoisted her off the ground and whirled her around, slamming her back against the side of the wagon. Air exploded from her lungs and the shock rattled through every bone in her body, but she began to laugh as he pulled back and set her down.

A hard grin spread over his lips. 'Sometimes I believe you enjoy the pain too much, my Catriona.'

The snake smile slithered on to her lips. 'Not half as much as I enjoy the pleasure. You know I like my men rough.'

'There is time for that later, pretty one. Now tell me, why have you returned so early?'

She frowned, wanting him right there and then, knowing the fever of danger rushing through her blood made her amorous and animalistic. She wondered if she frightened him the way he frightened her. Yes, she did; she could see it in his eyes. He was a brutal and unforgiving man, even more so a violent lover, yet still she could surpass him in her cruelty and depraved passion and that made him wonder how far she would go, whether she had moral limits. Good. She liked it that way.

'An old man came into town with his niece. He knows about the silver-mine.'

A black flame ignited in Junas's eyes and he stepped back, face going livid. 'How is this possible?'

'If I knew that I wouldn't have had to talk him into coming back tonight for a séance.'

'You say he knows of the mine and yet you toy with him, Catriona? Have you lost hold of your mind?'

That turned her blood to flame. A sudden urge to pluck the derringer from her bosom and blow a hole in his forehead almost overwhelmed her. 'Do not question me in that tone, Junas. You know I am more clever than you. He does not know where the mine is. After our little show tonight he will be no closer to it. In fact, he shall be much farther.'

Junas's eyes narrowed, anger raging, barely restrained. 'Too much is at stake to risk playing games. We must kill him.'

'We will do it *my* way. Killing the old man and his niece might attract the marshal and spoil our plans to get that saloon legitimately.'

'Then we kill the marshal as well.'

'Maybe we should just kill the whole goddamned town, eh?'

'I see no problem with that. I have wanted to kill the saloon man all along.'

'You are a buffoon, Junas. Kill him and any chance of him selling us that place cheap and legal-like goes out the window. You think they'd just hand it over to two gypsies?'

'I do not like it when you speak to me in such a way, Catriona. You should watch your vile tongue.'

Anger surged into her veins but she held it in check. Junas was an imbecile, but useful for the time being. He knew silver and was as powerful as a bear. She was not about to dig the ore out by herself.

Sliding a beguiling look on to her lips, she pressed into his arms. She could handle him and his overzealous urge for murder as long as it suited her purpose. As she would handle the old man and his niece tonight by sending them looking for a non-existent mine in some other part of Colorado Territory. Until then, she had needs and Junas was going to fulfill them, willing or not . . .

★ ★ ★

What the hell was Phidias thinking, asking some saloon gypsy fortune-teller for help? Was he so desperate to find that stupid mine, one that looked less and less likely to exist, that he had started to believe in spook talkers?

Grace's blood boiled as she strode down the boardwalk. She had worried all along that this silver-mine excursion would turn out to be just another one of his loco dreams, but she had hoped that just this once it would pan out and allow an old man the fulfillment he craved to leave this life in peace.

Leave this life?

The thought pricked her, made emotion tighten her throat, and threatened to send tears spilling from her eyes. She hadn't wept in years and she simply would not allow herself that luxury now. She refused to accept the fact Phid was telling her something, something vital and something that meant an end to his life faster than she reckoned she was ready to face.

Selfish. Sometimes she could be such, and she sure as hell was now. She didn't want him to go. Even knowing full well this mine would likely never pan out she had insisted on accompanying him. She would have gone anywhere with him just to avoid being alone. But that was inevitable, wasn't it? Hell, no man would be attracted to her south-of-feminine nature and she certainly didn't make it a lick easier for them to court her. Even that marshal, whom she had to admit caught her fancy; she had managed to alienate him in no time flat. Why did she always push folks away? Was she so afraid to let someone close, let someone . . . *love her*?

Christ ridin' a donkey, what was she

thinking? Love wasn't for her anyway and she wasn't scared of nothin'. No sirree. Not her, not Grace Crowly.

She stopped, emotion making her shudder. She scolded herself for thinking such thoughts and letting herself get all sentimental. Jesus H., life was life and it was going to happen no matter how much she refused to let it. The Lord did what He damn well wanted and that was that. The Almighty had taken her parents and now He would take Phid and laugh in the face of her tears. Lord of Mercy and Kindness? *Pfft*! Not in her life.

She reprimanded herself for the blasphemous thought. Why the hell did she feel so contrary sometimes? Phid was right, though she'd never tell him so. So much conflict raged inside her, so much . . . fear?

That word again. One to be denied. She wasn't afeared of anything or anyone.

Not ever.

A nagging feeling inside told her she

was lying to herself. Again.

With a curse, she started forward, taking slower steps and deeper breaths. Some of the anger ebbed from her being. She supposed she couldn't fault the old man for grasping at intangibles. He was simply reaching for anything that proved he wasn't just a fool and hadn't been rooked by a dying old buzzard without a penny to his name. El Silverado. A saloon. Not a silvermine. Didn't it just figure. Perhaps better than nothing, but she knew Phid wouldn't want it. He wanted silver and the security he'd never had. Wanted it for her. She was stubborn and ornery and maybe more than a handful foolish in her own right but she could tell what he was thinking. Always could. He had come here to make a strike for her, not himself. He had come here to . . .

Die?

She couldn't bring herself to consider it. Another rush of emotion choked her throat and staggered her step. She stopped, briefly leaning against a building for support, struggling to force the feelings away.

A few beats later, when she looked up, she saw she had stopped before a dress shop, its window filled with gowns. Her sights settled on one in particular, a frivolous thing with blue frills and lace.

Not for her.

What the hell would she do with a dress like that, anyway? She had never worn such a garment, least not since she was a little girl and her ma had sewn her a pretty little easter dress. The same dress she had worn to their buryin', then stuffed into an old trunk, afraid to ever look at again because she would start bawling.

For long moments she couldn't take her gaze from the dress, a feeling of lonesomeness and missed chances haunting her.

'You don't mind my sayin' it, you'd look right pretty in that dress . . . '

The voice came from behind her and she jolted. She whirled, anger buzzing in her veins like hornets.

'What the hell you doin' sneakin' up on me that way?' she shouted at the marshal, who stood with one foot on the boardwalk, hat in hand. Deep in thought, she hadn't heard him approach and embarrassment made her legs want to shake.

'Wasn't sneakin'. Just got back from the trail and saw you admiring that dress. Was gonna find you and your uncle and tell you what I discovered 'bout your shooter.'

The muscles on either side of her jaw knotted. 'Well, you could have made more noise or something.'

'Want to try it on?'

'What?' Heat surged through her face.

'The dress. Owner's a friend of mine and I'm sure she wouldn't mind.'

'You're right forward, ain't you?'

'Not usually, but I saw the look on your face and figured I'd offer.'

'You can go figure somewhere else. I don't wear dresses.'

He nodded, appeared momentarily

taken aback and she was glad. Served him right for catching her off guard that way.

A thin smile crossed his lips. 'Maybe you should.'

'What the hell business is it of yours?'

'Cussin' ain't attractive on a woman.' His eyes narrowed. Hell, he was right handsome and she grew annoyed with herself for thinking such a thought.

'Neither is righteousness on a man.'

'You sure you don't want to try on the dress?' He ignored her barb and that got under her skin. She expected a reaction when she insulted a fella.

'I could never afford something like that and don't rightly belong in it anyway. Not that it's a lick of your business.'

'Where's your uncle?' He raised an eyebrow. She suppressed the urge to kick him in the teeth.

'Hell, last I saw he was in the saloon thinkin' about asking a damn gypsy to help him . . . ' She caught herself before she finished blurting out the reason they had come to Silver Bluff.

'Help him what?'

'Help him find out who shot at us.' She said it without missing a beat but a hint of suspicion crossed the marshal's features.

'I'll find him there, I reckon.' He set his hat on his head and her eyes narrowed.

'I took myself a walk first. He might not be there no more. Why you want him anyway?'

'Wanted to tell you both what I found on the trail and ask him a few questions.'

'S'pose you tell me what you found and I'll tell him for you.'

He grinned. 'Found someone shot at you.'

'Well, no kidding, lawdog. You musta got that from the gypsy.'

'You got a right prickly way to you, ma'am.'

Anger danced a two-step in her belly. 'Thought I told you where you could put that ma'am stuff.'

He laughed but it carried an edge of irritation. She smiled, pleased with herself.

'Found a Winchester casing and some tracks someone tried to brush away. Whoever it was had already left, though. Doubt they'll bother you again.'

She caught a hint of skepticism in his voice. He didn't doubt it. In fact, he wondered if there were more to the shooting, and he was likely right.

'Hope you're right.'

' 'Less there's somethin' more you want to tell me? Was figuring on askin' your uncle, but since you're bein' so co-operative . . . '

'Get lost is all I can think of.'

He frowned, looking slightly hurt and a twinge of guilt pricked her. Christamighty, there she went again, pushing away someone who might genuinely be trying to help.

'You see your uncle, tell him I want to talk to him. If not, I'll find him myself.' He turned to walk away and she felt a sudden urge to make him stop, stay a while longer.

'Marshal?' she said haltingly and he turned back to her.

'Yes?'

She hesitated, unsure why she had even called to him. 'Nothing, Marshal. Nothing at all.' With that she whirled and strode down the boardwalk, not looking back and giving herself a chance to change her mind about confiding in a man she had only met a short while ago, but one for whom she felt a blossoming attraction. Hell, contrary she was, indeed.

4

Phidias Crowly fell to his knees beside the stream and peered into the bubbling water. Sunlight glazed its surface with a glassy sheen; topaz jewels sparkled their way downstream. The water's murmuring calmed some of the turmoil eating away his insides, but not enough to quell the crushing suspicion he had again bet his life on a bluff. A silver bluff.

He had let Grace down. There was no silver-mine. El Silverado was a saloon. A worthless one, to him at any rate, stuck out in the middle of nowhere. He had no use for a bar and neither did Grace. El Silverado was the final defeat in a life abundant with failures.

The realization hit like a mule kick, though he should have rightly expected the results, and, perhaps, in some shunned corner of his mind, had. The road to Hell wasn't paved with good intentions; it was paved with silver.

A shuddering sigh rattled his bony frame; or was it a sob? Hell, what did it matter? No one was out there to see it anyway. Reaching out with trembling fingers and trembling soul, he touched the water.

A bit chilly, it brought a shiver to his being, or, perhaps, that was simply despair working deeper into his soul. Vision blurring, for a frozen moment he reckoned he saw Millie's face shimmer within the flow, smiling her polished-silver smile, the smile she always saved for him alone, even when he royally mussed things up. He missed her. Lordamighty, he missed her.

'When I promised Grace's ma and pa I'd look after her if anything ever happened to them, I never really thought that day would come, Millie . . . ' The words came mumbled, uttered in private to a memory that was always close, yet always distant. He lifted his head, swallowed hard, eyes glassy with the threat of tears. 'I didn't reckon it would be so hard raisin' a child. I made her too much like me, Millie. She's got the wanderlust in her blood. Got it bad. I wanted more for her, I truly did. I wanted her life to be better than mine. She deserves the best and all I'll be leavin' her with is dust.' A tear wandered from his eye and words bunched in his throat. The whiskey was making him maudlin as hell but he reckoned an old man with nothing to his name was permitted a weak moment or two.

'I miss you, Millie. I miss you in a powerful way. I'll be joinin' you soon, but I got one more thing left to do before I come to you. I gotta make sure Grace has a chance. I reckon I don't know how right now . . . I reckon I don't know much of anything. Never did.' He uttered a thin laugh. 'Hell of a time to figger that out, ain't it?'

He waited for her to answer, the way he had a thousand times before. But no answer came. Hell, she was gone. What did he expect?

Grace was right: he was a crazy old bastard. He knew she didn't mean it; it was just her way of hidin' the fact she was scared, but it was on the mark just the same.

A stabbing pain lanced his chest and he gasped, pitching forward and nearly falling into the stream. A vise clamp squeezed his ribs and slivers of hot iron radiated across his shoulders and through his upper back.

Not now, please, not now . . .

He clutched his chest, struggling to suck in a breath of spring air, calm himself, but the pain only increased. Shivers of numbness swept down his left arm. Sweat beaded on his forehead and streamed down his weathered features, dripping off his mustache. Blood deserted his face, giving his skin an ashen pallor. With all his strength, he tried to reach his feet, failing, collapsing back to his knees.

Images began to whirl in his mind,

flashes of scenes from his life with Millie: a church social, her wearing a gingham gown he'd bought her for their third anniversary, and Grace as a little girl, a bitter fragile thing who'd not come out of the kitchen corner for two days after her folks passed.

Just as quickly the cascade of memories dissolved and the pain in his chest ebbed, leaving him trembling, gasping, drenched with sweat. His heart settled into its normal rhythm, if a bit accelerated. The tingling in his arm faded.

You got lucky that time. Lord almost took ya, you old fool. Serves you right for smokin' that cigar and drinkin' that whiskey. You know better.

Drawing shallow breaths, he tried to calm himself. What little strength he had returned and he forced himself to his feet. Legs rubbery, he stood, staring out at the water, as if another piece of his soul had just washed away.

★ ★ ★

'What the goddamn hell's he doin' — prayin'?' Reb Parker's brow furrowed as he peered downward.

Orville shook his head, a slightly puzzled expression turning his face. No, Crowly wasn't praying. Something was wrong with him, way he grabbed his chest and swayed. Old man's ticket was ready for punching, by the looks of it.

They stood on a ridge overlooking the stream, concealed behind a stand of fir. The mute hardcase stood back about twenty feet, leaning against an aspen, arms locked. About to head back to the camp, Orville had heard the old man ride up and stayed to watch him dismount and fall to his knees by the stream.

Orville's voice came cold and low. 'Gonna take more than prayin' to find that mine.'

Reb let out a scoffing grunt. 'Hell, ain't no mine. He's just loco.'

Orville cast the hardcase a threatening glare. 'I ask for your opinion?' An edge sharpened his tone, one that said

90

damn little stood between Reb and a hot piece of lead.

Parker scowled and looked down at the old man kneeling by the water. 'We best just kill him and be done with it.'

'Let him find the mine first. Won't be long 'fore he dies on his own, anyway.'

'Looks like he's about to now.'

Orville's gaze narrowed and he watched the old man reel, attempt to stand, then collapse back to his knees. His gaze remained intent until Crowly brought himself under control. A small sigh of relief escaped his lips after the old man recovered. If the old bastard died now it would make finding that mine more difficult and Orville wasn't one to tolerate unnecessary hardship.

A dark doubt rose in his mind and the urge to put lead in Parker for seeding it there made him nearly draw his gun. What if the mine *was* just another one of the old man's foolish quests? Lord knew Crowly had come to Orville enough times over the years, beggin' for funding for whatever crazy scheme to find gold or silver he got in his mind. But this time Crowly had actually brought a title and map. When he'd financed the old man by calling in some favors he'd believed for once Crowly was on to something, something that would solve all Orville Wilkins's financial problems. Yet things weren't looking so good. And goddammit he hadn't come all this way to be the owner of a damn saloon in some nowhere town.

A sound broke his reverie and his gaze shifted down the trail. A rider was coming from town and Orville let out a curse.

'Christ, it's that marshal again.' Parker's voice snapped like a blacksnake.

'What the hell's he doin' back here?' Orville edged back behind the fir boughs to make sure he wasn't spotted.

'I'm tellin' ya, he's trouble. Just let me deal with him.'

Parker had a point. What reason did the marshal have for coming back this way? Had something in his first search aroused his suspicions?

'Much as I'm inclined to agree, killin' a lawman ain't the same as killin' an old man no one cares about. We don't need that kind of attention right now.'

'This town's in the middle of goddamned nowhere. Who'll be able to do anything about it?' Parker shook his head, the smug expression on his face irritating the hell out of Orville.

Orville removed his derby and ran a hand over his pomaded hair, considering Reb's words, but caution got the better of him. They could always deal with the lawdog later, if it became certain he was going to interfere with the operation.

'Just hold off for now, Parker. Ain't no point in pokin' a sleeping bear in the ribs.'

'You're a fool, Wilkins,' muttered Parker and Orville's belly tightened with anger. Gaze pinning the man, eyes narrowing, a blood lust washed over him. Parker took notice and moved sideways a few feet, wary of being clacked in the jaw a second time with Orville's Smith & Wesson.

Orville glanced back at the mute hardcase, who appeared unconcerned with the exchange. Orville suddenly wished Parker was mute as well. Dumb men didn't grouse and he'd damn near reached his limit of Parker's belly-aching and questioning of his authority. It wouldn't take much more before he shut the hardcase's mouth permanently.

★　★　★

An hour after talking to Grace, Jim Morgan guided his horse on to the trail leading out of town. He had decided to have a powwow with Crowly and ask the old man to tie up a few loose ends. He'd tried the saloon first but the 'keep informed him Crowly had left within the half-hour. Checking with Mrs Philbert, he learned the prospector hadn't retired to the boardinghouse, either. After questioning a couple townsfolk lounging in chairs on the boardwalk, Morgan learned Crowly had headed towards the trail. The old man's actions struck him as risky, considering he had been shot at a short time earlier at the very place he was headed, but maybe Crowly didn't figure he was in any real danger.

Whatever the case, the more he thought over the shooting incident the more his lawdog instincts told him Crowly needed to answer some questions about his business here in Silver Bluff.

The irony of the situation struck him. Hours earlier he'd been grousing about Silver Bluff being a peaceful town where nothing untoward ever happened. Now he was up to his ears investigating a shooting mystery. The thought of it made the blood rush in his veins.

Or is it her that makes your blood rush, Morgan?

Why did he want to deny the fact that Grace Crowly had indeed gotten under his skin in a way that wasn't totally unpleasant? Maybe he was just too damn gun-shy after what Lady Wescott had done to him. Still, he caught himself trying to imagine how Grace would look wearing that blue dress, her hair down and maybe a smile on a face that he reckoned smiled far too infrequently. Was there a softness hidden beneath her tough exterior? In front of the shop he thought he had sensed a troubled spirit dwelling beneath her abrasive posture.

Why do you care? She'd just bite your hand off if you held it out anyhow.

Grace Crowly was no gal to settle down with, even if she were interested. And as Lady Wescott so gracefully pointed out, he didn't make nearly enough as a small town lawman to even think about supporting a wife and family.

He sat straight up in the saddle, fingers clenching the reins tighter. *Wife?* Hell, who said anything about a wife? What the devil made him think something like that?

Shaking his head, he drew up and peered about at the woodland and steep hills. Sunlight shimmered through boughs like shivering emeralds. Birds twittered and the gurgling rush of the stream came from his right. On any other day the peacefulness of the scene might have unearthed feelings of boredom and a craving for something more exciting. Now it suddenly made him pause in awe, appreciate the serenity of nature and the rugged grandeur of the forest. For the life of him he couldn't figure out what had changed. A surge of euphoria mixed with confusion accompanied the thoughts; he wondered whether it came from excitement at the prospect of real law work, or if it had more to do with a mule-headed spitfire of a gal with an Arkansas toothpick tongue?

Shaking the feeling, he heeled his horse into a slow walk and scanned the stream-bank for any sign of Crowly. A few hundred feet on, he spotted the old man kneeling by the edge of the water. Crowly appeared oblivious to Jim's approach, preoccupied. Slowing, Jim observed him a moment, watched him gain his feet and begin to turn, only to stop in mid-twist as his eyes settled on Jim's horse.

Reining up, Jim stepped from the saddle and led the mount up to the old man.

'Marshal . . . ' Crowly's voice sounded a hell of a lot weaker than it had in the office and Jim studied the man. Crowly's complexion was the color of hoar-frost. Sweat soaked his collar and dripped from his mustache. The old man took faltering steps and Jim wasn't entirely sure the fellow wouldn't collapse.

'You need help?' Jim cocked an eyebrow.

'Hell, why would I need help?' The old man's voice carried too much snap; he was lying.

'You don't look so good, Crowly, and you ain't walkin' none too straight.'

'Jest leave me be, will ya? Don't need

your damn help. Don't need nobody's help. What're you doin' here, anyway? Can't a fella go off in peace without bein' bothered?'

Jim's gaze narrowed. Crowly was doing a damn poor job of concealing his condition. Something was wrong with him and Jim aimed to find out what. 'Came lookin' for you. Some folks in town said you headed this way.'

'None of their goddamn business where I go, way I see it.'

Jim almost smiled. 'You're startin' to sound like that cactus-mouthed niece of yours.'

Crowly frowned, as if realizing he had been over-doing the gruff act. 'You're right. Reckon I was tryin' to come across that way.'

Jim uttered a strained laugh. 'Don't fit on you. Don't fit on her, neither, though I gotta admit she's right more practiced at it.'

'Grace's a good girl. She just ain't been around proper folks much. She ain't had an easy life.'

'Care to tell me about it?'

The old man cocked an eyebrow. 'That why you came lookin' for me, to hear her life story?'

Jim shrugged, looked at the ground, back to Crowly. 'No, reckon it ain't, but I'd like to know anyway.'

'Ain't a lot to tell. Her parents died in a cabin fire when she was a young'n. I promised them 'fore they went we'd raise her if anything happened, me and Millie. 'Cept Millie passed too and left me to raise her alone. Hell of a life for a young gal.'

'She don't seem to be complainin', least about that.' He smiled and the old man relaxed, some of the color bleeding back into his face.

Phidias Crowly blew out a long sigh, shoulders slumping. 'I'm a prospector, Marshal, one who spent his whole life searchin' for that one big strike. I dragged Grace along with me — well, maybe not dragged, because I reckon she's got wanderin' in her blood, too, but I feel responsible all the same.

Nothing ever panned out, not gold in California, silver in Arizona. All the while Grace, she missed out on the things a woman could teach her.'

'Reckon that was her choice. She don't look like the type to let anyone drag her where she don't want to go.'

'That don't make me feel any less responsible. She didn't have no choice in the early years.' A distant look drifted into his eyes. Jim felt sorry for him then. He saw a reflection of pain, loss, hopelessness in those cloudy eyes. Crowly was a man riding a last trail, and that trail was littered with the bones of unrealized dreams.

'Why'd you come to Silver Bluff, Mr Crowly?'

The old man glanced away, shifting feet, blinking. 'Just needed to get away for spell, is all.'

Jim scoffed. 'Hell, you're a damn poor liar, Crowly. S'pose you tell me the real reason.'

'Ain't no real reason. Just that.' Crowly's voice wavered.

Jim made no effort to conceal the doubt on his face. 'Like I told you in the office, Silver Bluff's normally a peaceful town. Now you two ride in and suddenly I got a shootin' that looks downright deliberate. I found tracks someone went to a hell of a lot of effort to brush away and a shell casing up on the ridge. Someone was firing at you, for a reason, Crowly. I want to know what that reason is.'

Crowly eyed him, defeat on his lined features. 'I can't give you that reason, Marshal. I jest got no answer to why someone would shoot at me or Grace. I got no enemies I can figure and Grace might have pissed off a hundred fellas for makin' advances at her but none to the point of wanting to kill her, least not yet.'

'Then s'pose you tell me what you do know and let me figure out the rest. You do realize someone tried to kill you — or doesn't your life matter any longer?'

A frown creased the prospector's lips.

'I reckon a bullet would make things a mite easier.'

'And I reckon that's the coward's way out.'

'You just don't understand, Marshal.' Crowly's frame seemed to shrink in on itself.

'Then tell me, Crowly. I think you want to. I think that's why you came to my office in the first place. And even if you want to die, you don't want that for Grace.' Jim locked his gaze with Crowly's, compassion on his features.

'I don't want to die, Marshal. I got no choice.' Crowly shook his white-tufted head. 'Sawbones in Texas told me I had maybe a year if I took real good care of myself and gave up whiskey and cigars. My ticker's quittin' on me.'

Jim swallowed hard, a chill settling over him. 'That why you looked so pale when I rode up?'

Crowly nodded. 'Had me a spell, a bad one. Thought I was goin' right there and then.'

'And you figure a bullet would spare you that?' Crowly didn't answer, but it was written across his face. 'I figure that would just deprive your niece of whatever time you got left.'

Crowly shook his head. 'She's better off without me. I feel powerful guilty, Marshal, guilty about too many things to mention, but mostly about not being able to leave Grace something more than I had in my life, which is plumb nothin'.'

Jim twisted the reins in his fingers. The old man's words made his belly cinch and for a moment Grace's face was in his mind, sick with grief. 'You got more than most folks, Mr Crowly. You got Grace. She's a tough gal. She'll make out when you gone, but I'm bettin' she had her choice she'd want the time you got left.'

Crowly uttered a feeble laugh. 'She won't even admit to herself I'm goin', though any fool could see I ain't long for this world. I have to leave something for her, Marshal. I have to.'

'That why you came to Silver Bluff?'

Crowly hesitated, then reached into his pocket. 'I reckon it won't matter after tonight who knows. Secret will be out anyway.' He drew out two pieces of folded parchment paper, handed them to Morgan. 'I took the title and map out of Grace's saddle-bags in case she didn't want to give them back to me later.'

Jim flipped open the map. His brow knotted. 'El Silverado?' He looked up at Crowly, understanding dawning on his face. 'You came to Silver Bluff searching for a little-known fable?'

'Well, we came looking for the mine at any rate. The town was a bit of a surprise.' Crowly explained how the old man had given him the map and title on his deathbed. Jim listened intently, not quite knowing what to make of it.

'That silver-mine was always a legend and a minor one at that. No one ever found it and damn few bothered lookin'.'

Crowly shrugged. 'I figured it was my last chance to give Grace the life she deserved.'

Jim handed the map and title back to the old man. 'You tell anyone else about this? Show the map to anyone?'

Crowly nodded. 'Just my cousin, Orville Wilkins. He financed the trip, though don't tell Grace that. She rightly can't stand his hide since she was a young'un.'

Jim's expression turned thoughtful. 'Wonder if that might not explain who was shootin' at you . . . '

'Hell, Orville?' The old man's brow crinkled. 'He ain't got no notion where I was goin'. No one could read that map 'cept me. 'Sides, if I find the mine he knows I'll pay him back plus extra.'

Jim wasn't so sure Orville could be ruled out. 'You tell anyone else?'

'No . . . no, just him.'

'Name of the mine on your title's the same as the saloon . . . '

'Fact didn't escape me, Marshal. I'm afraid I might have left Grace a whiskey parlor instead of a silver-mine.'

Jim sighed. 'Truth remains someone took a shot at you, Mr Crowly and that someone had a reason. Way I see it, there ain't much better reason than a lode of silver.'

'An you figure that someone might be Orville?'

Jim nodded. 'Orville or maybe someone he told.'

'Well, he's fixin' to be disappointed. All I got is a saloon and I don't want it. Grace won't either.'

Jim studied the man, wondering if he were telling everything this time and deciding he likely was. 'You said after tonight it wouldn't be a secret. What'd you mean by that?'

Crowly let out a brittle laugh. 'Just that I'm havin' me a parley with the spirit folks tonight at the saloon.'

'Madam Catriona?'

'Yep, she overheard me and Grace fussin' and offered to ask the spirits to tell me where the mine is.'

A doubtful look crossed Jim's face. 'You don't rightly believe that, do you?'

'Well, no, but I figure any chance's worth takin' and she is a right purty gal.

What have I got to lose?'

'Likely a handful of silver dollars.' Jim offered a thin smile. Was that all there was to it? Was that gypsy merely looking to part an old man from his money? Most likely, though perhaps Grace would be attending and it would give him a chance to . . . before he could think about it his mouth was working. 'Reckon if you're fixed on it I'll join you tonight.'

Crowly grinned and Jim wondered if the old man had read his thoughts. 'You got some spirits you want to talk to?'

'Only spirits in that saloon come out of bottles. Fact is, I been wonderin' why those gypsies haven't moved on. Ain't much in the way of payin' prospects here, though at least folks are friendly towards them. Just want a chance to see her act first hand.'

'You sure you just don't want a chance to see Grace again?'

A wave of heat swept across Jim's cheeks and he reckoned he couldn't hide the red on his face. 'Ain't got nothin' to do with it, Mr Crowly.'

Crowly uttered an easy laugh. 'Hell, I was guessin', but by the look on your face . . . '

Jim turned to his horse and stepped into the saddle, cursing himself for betraying his thoughts, even ones half-formed. 'We best be headin' back. Don't need to give whoever shot at you another chance.'

Crowly nodded. 'Won't argue with you there, Marshal.' He started towards his horse, which was tethered to a branch a few feet away, then turned. 'Oh, Marshal . . . '

Jim looked directly at him, unable to shake his embarrassment totally. 'Yeah?'

'Grace's a hell of a gal. She comes across tough as old jerky but her heart's soft as silk.'

Jim gripped the reins tighter. 'I'll escort you back, Mr Crowly. She's like to be worried by now.'

Crowly uttered a laugh that said he was getting a big kick out of Jim's discomfort. Morgan didn't much appreciate it, but kept his mouth shut and swung his horse in the direction of town.

* * *

With the dusk a chill came to the air. Hanging lanterns in front of shops cast a cidery light and shadows thickened and bunched. As Jim Morgan made his way along the boardwalk to the saloon, the whole thought of communicating with spirits struck him as ludicrous. After what Crowly had told him about wanting the silver-mine for Grace, the notion of some sideshow gypsy bilking him out of money got under Jim's skin, but it wasn't his decision. It was Crowly's, and likely it was another misstep in a long line of them. If the situation hadn't been so serious he might have laughed, especially if he added to the mix the 'keep's constant grumbling about his saloon being haunted.

His mind shifted to Crowly's confession at the stream. Considering what the prospector aimed to find in Silver Bluff, the motive was plain, in Jim's estimation. The brushed-over tracks and shell casing indicated the shot was deliberate and likely a danger remained. But why hadn't the sniper followed up the shot? Why hadn't he killed Crowly and Grace right there and then? A mistake? A mistimed shot? An attempt to frighten? For what reason?

Crowly had shown his cousin the map and title. That was the only link Jim could connect, unless the old man was holding back information. Assuming he had told all, either Orville Wilkins or someone Wilkins had hired was likely on the prospector's trail.

Mind returning to the gypsy, he wondered whether she had a stake in it beyond parting the old man and a few pieces of change. Did she believe his silver-mine story? If she did, was she looking to somehow swindle the old man out of his title?

He shook his head, dismissing the notion for the moment. Those gypsies had arrived in Silver Bluff seven months ago; though opportunistic, he doubted they'd have much interest in a mine. They were performers, not miners, and getting silver out of rock wasn't as simple as taking it out of an old man's pocket.

Unless he discovered facts proving otherwise he couldn't stop the fortune-teller from running her show. The notion pricked at his sense of decency, but Crowly had a right to throw his money away if he so desired.

What about Grace's right?

She had made her choice to accompany him, follow a silver-dust trail leading nowhere, but Crowly hadn't told her all the facts where Wilkins was concerned. Did that change anything? While she had a right to know, it wasn't Jim's place to tell her. He reckoned she would have never let her uncle go searching for the mine on his own even with the knowledge.

The thought of the young woman brought a resurgence of the confusion and excitement he'd felt earlier on the trail, despite all attempts to suppress it. Something about the gal put starch in his stride. Even Crowly had noticed it.

Jim halted suddenly, for the second time today gripped by an undeniable sensation of being watched. Turning, he scanned the boardwalk. Nothing but creeping shadows and patches of shifting murk met his gaze. The street was deserted except for an occasional shopkeep locking up and heading out for the night.

But for the briefest of moments he could have sworn someone was observing him, following. Maybe the notion of séances and spirit folk had just tightened his nerves more than he supposed. Casting the street a final look, he muttered, 'Relax, Morgan. You wanted a break from the mundane, now you got it. Don't start gettin' all jumpy over shadows.'

He let a smile filter across his lips and started to turn, halting as he realized he stood before the dress-shop window. His gaze settled on the garment Grace had been admiring. His smile widened as he recollected the longing in her eyes as she looked at that dress, a longing somehow childlike in its innocence. And regretful. She had told him she couldn't afford it and that it didn't belong on her. The first was an excuse, the second just plain wrong.

She belonged in that dress. And part of her knew it, and was perhaps frightened by the fact. He could imagine how lovely she would . . .

Christ, stop it!

Hell, he'd let his thoughts run loose again. If she was too pig-headed to be honest about her wants what was it to him?

Nothing.

With a dismissing wave of his hand, he resumed his walk towards the El Silverado. Reaching the saloon, he pushed through the batwings. Low-turned lanterns made the interior murky, and a heavy cloud of Durham smoke swirled in the air. No patrons sat at the tables and a velvet curtain had been draped over the back wall and door, directly behind the gypsy's table. An anemic flame fluttered from a candle placed in the table's center.

Jim plucked his hat from his head and went to the bar, where Phidias Crowly perched on a stool. The old man looked a mite better than he had by the stream but far from healthy.

Grace sat beside him, frame rigid, a sour expression saddled to her lips.

The barkeep busied himself wiping out glasses and setting them beneath the counter, but his flittery manner telegraphed the message he was less than thrilled with the possibility of having spooks visiting his saloon instead of customers.

'Evenin', Marshal,' Crowly said.

Jim nodded, then peered at Grace. 'Miss Crowly.'

Phidias offered a weak smile. 'She ain't in the best of minds, Marshal. She don't much cotton to the idea of spirit talks.'

Grace scowled. 'I been tellin' the crazy old coot this ain't nothin' but a waste of silver. He's got his pecker in a twist on account of that gypsy tramp — '

Crowly reddened. 'Grace, please! Don't make this any harder than it is already. I rightly told you I didn't put much stock in séances but I figure it's worth a chance.'

'Ain't worth spooks in my saloon,' the 'keep put in, a hitch in his voice. 'Just make sure they leave with ya.'

Grace gave an exasperated *pfft*. 'Dammit, I told you there ain't no such things as spooks.'

'Beg to differ, ma'am,' the 'keep said and Grace's eyes flamed.

'You call me ma'am one more time and you'll find out first hand if there's such.' She glared at the 'keep, who backed away, using what Jim considered was sensible judgement.

'Where's the gypsy?' Jim nudged his head towards the table.

'She said promptly at six,' Crowly said. ''Bout two minutes to go.'

'Dark outside. Reckon that's what she was waitin' on.'

Crowly nodded. 'She told the 'keep to turn out all the lanterns. Just wanted that little candle. Said the spirits don't like too much light.'

Grace made a disgusted sound and slid off her stool. 'Let's get this charade over with, Phid. I'm coddlin' the urge to throttle that gal if she don't hurry it up.'

Crowly chuckled and Jim went to the lanterns, extinguishing them in turn. The barkeep shuffled over to the table, reluctance in his stride, and took a seat. Crowly followed suit. Grace muttered something Jim had never heard come out of a woman, but slid into a chair. Jim took the seat between the 'keep and Grace, figuring it would stave off any trouble between the two. The candle flickered and cast eerie jumping shadows about the table.

A creak sounded and Jim knew somebody was opening the door behind the curtain. He noted it didn't close and he bet he knew why. Her partner would likely wait behind that doorway with any number of performance-enhancing parlor tricks.

The curtains parted and the gypsy woman stepped through with almost laughable dramatics. A deep-blue velvet robe covered her body. She gazed at them each in turn for effect. Another urge to laugh came over him, but he managed to suppress it. Her hands went to the sash holding her robe together and she tugged on the ends. The sash undone, she slipped the robe from her shoulders and let it crumple into a pile at her feet.

Crowly gulped and let out a choked sound.

'What the hell's wrong with *you*?' Grace asked, though the answer was obvious.

'She . . . she's nekked.' Crowly's voice fluttered and he licked his lips.

'What's the matter, ain't you never seen a naked gal before?' For the first time Jim caught the hint of a laugh in

Grace's voice and it sounded right becoming on her.

'Been a spell . . . ' Crowly muttered, eyes wide.

Catriona smiled, obviously pleased with the effect she was having on the old man, as well as the 'keep, whose gaze was glued to her ample bosom. Jim's own mouth went dry at the sight of the nude woman. The Good Lord had been right generous the day he passed out curves to Catriona.

'There should be no barriers between the flesh and the spirit world,' Catriona said as she settled into her chair. Her speech carried a peculiar muffled quality, Jim noted.

'I'm inclined to agree.' A boyish smirk played on Crowly's lips.

'Dirty old buzzard!' Grace snapped.

'We must all join hands. Let no one break the circle once it is formed.' Catriona placed her hands on the table and the 'keep took one, Crowly the other.

Jim joined hands with the bartender

119

and Grace. The young woman's hand felt soft, more delicate than he would have expected, given her rough ways. With a strange shiver, he reckoned he could grow used to holding her hand all too easy.

Catriona's head lowered; she appeared to be staring at the table. Seconds dragged and Jim waited for the theatrics to commence. A clanking sounded, its direction indistinct, but if he had to guess he would have pin-pointed it as coming from beneath the floor to his left. That puzzled him. He'd expected something from behind the curtain.

The clanking echoed again, a series of muffled plinks, and he suddenly realized what the sound brought to mind — a miner's pick hitting stone. He reckoned that's exactly what he was supposed to think.

A gasp came from the 'keep and Jim felt the man's fingers tighten uncomfortably on his own.

'I told ya this place had spooks. Them's the sounds I been hearing.' The barman's voice jittered.

Grace glanced at the gypsy. 'Like hell! Spooks in wolf's clothing, if you ask me.'

'Shush!' Crowly ordered with a hiss and Grace clamped her mouth shut. The pinched look on her face said she was downright steamed at being quieted.

The clanking ceased as Catriona uttered a low moan. Her head swayed from side to side, then forward, back, and finally in a circular motion. Jim reckoned this was the part where she pretended to go into a trance. He had seen it before; he recollected Lady Wescott had believed in such nonsense and dragged him to parlors in Austin where psychics pretended to be possessed by spirits of the dead. Granted, Catriona was a whole lot more lovely and a whole lot more naked, but it boiled down to the same thing: they were all con men, in his estimation.

'Phidias Crowly . . . ' Her voice came out half moan, half words.

The old man's gaze jerked up; he had been staring at her cleavage.

'I'm right here.' Crowly's voice jumped out, laced with a note of awe, as if he were completely falling for her routine.

'You will not find your mine here, Phidias Crowly.' Her voice still sounded muffled, but deeper.

'And just who do you think you are to say that?' The words came with a sharp challenge and Grace half-rose out of her seat. Jim tightened his grip on her hand and she settled back on to the chair.

'I am the voice of the lost miner . . . ' The gypsy made it sound so serious it was laughable. As fortune-teller performances went this was pretty typical, even clichéd, but he suspected more people paid to see a naked gypsy than any ghost show.

'You'll be more than lost if you don't stop this horseflop.' Grace pulled at his grip but he held fast. He didn't want her stopping the show at this point; he wanted to see just how far the gypsy would go, and why.

'The mine is forty miles due east, at the outskirts of a town called Brownville.' Catriona swayed, lips barely moving as words came out. 'I died trying to mine its silver.'

He had expected her to dance around the mine's location, but she appeared to be trying to steer Crowly away from town altogether. Did that mean she had more of an interest in the mine than he previously thought?

Jim's gaze swept over the tense faces around the table. The idea hadn't dawned on Crowly yet and the barkeep appeared too boogered to care. Only Grace's face registered suspicion.

'You must leave this place, Phidias Crowly. Ride to Brownville and claim your fortune . . . ' Her mouth suddenly opened wide and a strand of some whitish substance flowed from between her teeth. The substance was gauzy, vaguely serpentlike in the low light. It snaked from her mouth and dropped into her lap.

'What the hell is that?' Grace's eyes widened and for once she appeared unnerved.

Jim frowned. 'Sideshow tellers call it ectoplasm, spirit stuff.' He reckoned Catriona must have concealed it in her mouth the entire time, dislodging it with her tongue when needed. That explained her muffled tone. Despite her silly dramatics, the fortune-teller was skilled at her art, which made him wonder all the more why she remained in a town like Silver Bluff when her act would have proven more lucrative elsewhere.

Something began to form in back of her then, something whitish and indistinct. It materialized from the folds of the curtain and swelled in size. White and flowing, it shaped into the vague outline of a figure.

Crowly let out a gasp and a name slipped through his lips in a whisper. 'Millie . . . '

Grace's hand tightened on Jim's and the angry look on her face turned to one of unadulterated fury. Crowly was plainly believing just what the gypsy hoped he would, that his dead wife had come from the spirit world, no doubt also to direct him away from Silver Bluff in case the miner's declaration proved insufficient. Jim studied the diaphanous figure. He could make out no real features, though the thing would be taken for a woman in a night-gown, given its shape. The lighting made it impossible to tell anything further.

Crowly started to gasp. The bleached look on his face told Jim instantly the old man was experiencing more than just surprise at seeing the supposed spirit of his deceased wife. Sweat streamed from his forehead and his entire body trembled.

'Jesus H. Christ, you got a hell of a nerve!' yelled Grace, jerking her hand from Jim's grip and endeavoring to hurl herself across the table at the gypsy.

Jim wrapped an arm around the

young woman's waist and hauled her back, which was by no means an easy feat, considering how riled she was. He stood, his own anger rising. 'This has gone far enough — '

A thundering blast sounded and a flash of flame came from the batwings before Jim could make a grab for the 'ghost'. Searing pain sliced across his arm and lead plowed into the table, punching straight through in a spray of flying splinters.

Morgan knew if he hadn't been rising, the bullet would have likely gone through his back into a lung or worse. He staggered, thrown off balance by the shot. He tried to spin towards the doors while unlimbering his Colt.

The barkeep let out an unmanly bleat and Grace turned the air blue with a series of curses. The gypsy woman scrambled for her robe and gathered up the remains of her ectoplasm. The 'spirit' had vanished behind the curtain.

Whoever triggered the shot was gone by the time Jim managed to draw his gun and take a handful of steps towards the batwings.

'Get the lights on!' Morgan yelled. Grace had already grabbed a lantern. She had it lit an instant later. The barkeep jerked from his shock and attended to the other lamps.

'You OK?' Grace asked, and Jim wasn't sure whether he was more startled by the gunshot or the concern in her voice.

He nodded and she ran to Phidias, who was sitting in the chair looking pale, but breathing smoothly enough to tell Jim he was going to recover.

The gypsy tied her robe closed, likely concealing her ectoplasm beneath it.

Commotion settled, Jim started for the door.

'Where the hell *you* going?' Grace shouted and he turned to her. The worry in her eyes now as she held her uncle's hand softened her features considerably.

'After whoever fired at me. Might still be a chance of catching him.'

'I'll go with you.' She started towards him but he waved her back. 'It's my job, not yours. Tend to your uncle. He needs you.'

She appeared ready to argue but he gave her no opportunity. He ran to the batwings and eased through. Gaze scanning the darkened street, he searched for a sign of the escaping shooter, but saw no one. He let out a curse and started down the boardwalk, keeping his back to the buildings. He held the Peacemaker close to his cheek, eyes alert for any sign of movement. His heart pounded and he reckoned this was about as far from boredom as a body got. Maybe a peaceful town wasn't such a bad way to go after all.

Making his way along the boardwalk, he listened for any sound of running footsteps or a horse bolting into motion. Only the mocking whisper of the breeze reached his ears. Dust stirred, making a slithery scratching noise on the worn planks.

The shooter couldn't have escaped that fast. He had to be somewhere close by. Any number of places offered concealment: alleyways, wagons, barrels . . .

A flash of movement stopped the thought dead. Lantern-light glinted from metal across the street and a shot blasted from an alley. Jim pitched sideways and an instant later lead plowed into the wall, barely missing his head.

Before the bushwhacker had a chance to adjust his aim, Jim dove for the shelter of a rain barrel. A second shot rang out. The bullet punched a hole straight through the barrel. Water spouted on to the boards.

Running. Heavy bootfalls pounded the hardpack.

Chancing a look, he saw a man bolting from the alley into the street, heading for a horse tethered a hundred yards down, next to a second mount.

Jim leaped from behind the barrel, Peacemaker arcing up. He triggered a shot, but had no chance to aim. The bullet missed, burying itself in the dirt. The man spun, murder visible on his face even in the poor light. A hardcase.

The man jerked up his gun and fired. Jim lunged sideways, sweeping his own gun around. The would-be killer's bullet went wide, the shot hurried, ill-aimed, and Jim triggered two shots. The first missed by a good six inches, but the second punched into the man's leg. The hardcase staggered, grunting and gripping his thigh with his free hand. Blood streamed between his fingers.

Jim started forward, steps cautious, keeping the Colt leveled on the fellow. The man glanced up and Jim saw intent glare in his eyes.

His belly plunged. 'Don't! You're a dead man if you try it.'

'You think so, you lawdog sonofabitch?' The man's gun was in motion even as the words came from his mouth. An old trick and a professional one.

Instinct taking over, Jim's finger twitched and the Peacemaker blasted. Lead plowed into the man's chest and sent him skipping backward.

The hardcase slammed into the dirt face first and lay still. Jim let out the breath he'd been holding, grimness washing over him. He had never killed a man, and though he had been given no choice it raised a rushing swell of nausea in his belly.

He went to the body and knelt, then turned the man on to his back. No one he recognized. He doubted the fella would prove to be Crowly's cousin but he would have the old man take a look at the body to make certain. He reckoned the man was responsible for the feeling of being watched he'd experienced on his way to the saloon.

Heaviness settling over him, he stood, holstering his Colt. He started back towards the saloon, only to stop as something struck him as wrong. At first he wasn't sure quite what, then it came to him.

The man had been heading towards his horse, and that horse had been next to another. His gaze fixed on the man's mount. One horse. The second animal was gone. Someone had silently led it off while he had been preoccupied with his regret over the hardcase's death. He was damn lucky he hadn't been killed, if the man was working with a partner, but the second man must have been more intent on guiding the horse out quietly than on starting a gunfight.

Drawing a deep breath, he went back to the saloon, feeling not only sick over the killing but foolish as well. When he entered, Grace was sitting next to Phidias Crowly, still holding his hand. The old man's face showed more color now but the barkeep looked pale as hell.

The gypsy woman was nowhere to be seen.

'He OK?' Jim ducked his chin at the prospector.

Grace nodded. 'He'll be fine, don't you worry about him.' The surliness was back in her voice and he found himself in no frame of mind to deal with it.

'Where'd Madam Ectoplasm get off to?'

Grace shrugged. 'She said all the commotion had ruined her spirit unity, whatever the hell that means, and went out through the back.'

Jim nodded and went to the curtain, sweeping it aside. The door was still open behind it and he saw no evidence of a ghost or anything remotely super-natural.

'What's back there?' He twisted his head to look back at the 'keep, who jolted as if slapped, apparently immersed in a trance of fear.

'Just a store room.'

Jim went through the doorway into a short hallway. At the end of the passage was a door that likely led to an alley. A second door stood to his left. Going to it, he gripped the glass handle and looked into the storeroom, which was cluttered with liquor — crates, a few barrels and shelves lined with cans. He gave the room a quick search, then closed the door. As his gaze scrutinized the short hallway, a notion took him. Wouldn't he have seen the gypsy woman come from the alley beside the saloon if she had gone out the back way? Most likely. She would have had to come out the front and walk down the boardwalk. Behind the saloon were hills thick with brush and forest, nearly impenetrable for a lone woman making her way back to the far end of town. That made her departure puzzling and the spook act look a hell of a lot more fishy than it did already. But did it connect her in any way to the shooter? He wasn't ready to go that far but he sure as hell would make a point to find out the next time she came into the saloon.

5

Orville Wilkins edged back behind a large aspen as hoofbeats pounded from down the trail. He knew it had to be his men returning from town but wasn't about to take any chances getting caught if that marshal came snooping around again. What the devil had taken them so long? Parker and the mute were only supposed to watch the séance and report back. They should have returned an hour ago. If that hardcase had blundered again . . .

Orville tensed suddenly and a chill moved down his spine as it dawned on him he heard only one set of hoofbeats. He squinted, peering downtrail, but he couldn't spot the rider yet; the darkness was too intense, even with a three-quarter moon. What if the marshal had caught Parker? Or worse, what if the *hombre* had created a commotion that led straight back Orville?

Muttering a curse, he reached a decision. Regardless of the outcome of the scouting expedition, the hardcase had out-lived his usefulness. Orville's hand drifted over the butt of his Smith & Wesson. 'There's a bullet with your name on it when you get back here, Parker . . . ' he said under his breath, jaw muscles knotting.

Ants crawling through his nerves, he concluded something else: he wasn't cut out for this kind of work. He was used to issuing orders from the comfort of his office, not traipsing through forests and dealing with hardcases. Following Crowly should have been an easy proposition, a quick pay-off. That's why he had trailed the old bastard himself instead of hiring men to do it for him, way he normally would. That and greed. The fewer who knew what he was after the smaller the distribution of proceeds. While he'd misjudged the particulars of the venture, the point might suddenly be moot, because the mine's very existence appeared in doubt. That was bad news, indeed. Certain creditors back in Texas would be inclined to nail Orville in a pine box if he didn't come up with the appreciable sum of money he owed them right quick. He needed that money yesterday. He was tired of waiting on that old man and he was goddamned fed up with mosquitoes and snakes and hot-headed hardcases who ignored orders. He had an empire to build, power to seize. He could see it in his mind: Wilkins Silver Enterprises. Founder of the largest strike this side of Leadville — *after* he paid back those men, of course, along with the piddly sums he owed to those with whom he'd called in favors to sponsor this expedition.

The sound of a horse snorting pulled him from his reverie. A twig snapped. He started and straightened, whirled to find the mute standing behind him, reins in hand. The man gave him a vacant stare, moonlight washing over his rough features and making him look like some spook raised at a séance.

'How the hell you come up here so quiet?' He tried to keep the wobble out of his tone, but failed.

The mute made a strangled sound half-way between a grunt and a squeak, which did little to help Orville's nerves.

'Where the hell is Parker? What took you so long?' Orville regained a measure of his composure, his carriage stiffening and his tone snapping with authority.

The mute's dark eyes narrowed and he drew a finger across his throat.

'You tellin' me he's dead?' Orville was unable to suppress a surge of annoyance. While he didn't care a lick about Parker's demise, he mourned the opportunity to perform the deed himself.

The mute nodded, patting the gun at his hip.

'He was shot? Marshal kill him?'

The mute nodded again and Orville sighed.

'Hell, reckon that means the fool

fired on him and attracted us some unwanted attention.' The mute nodded a third time. Orville cursed Parker, wishing he could put an extra bullet into the man's hide for good measure. Any stealth he'd intended was now shot to hell, literally. That meant it was time to change tactics.

'We best step things up.' He eyed the mute, whose expression remained placid. 'That old man's gonna find that silver-mine for me and he's gonna do it quick like . . .'

The mute spread his hands in a questioning gesture and mouthed the word, 'How?'

Orville laughed. 'Come dawn you sneak into Silver Bluff and keep an eye out for Grace Crowly. Follow her. When you get her alone, grab her with the least amount of noise. Bring her up to the camp. I'll write a note to the old man and you leave it where he or that marshal's likely to notice. He'll find that silver-mine a hell of a lot faster if I have his niece.'

139

A smile turned the mute's thick lips and his eyes seemed to glitter. He plainly liked the idea, maybe a bit too much, Orville reckoned.

'You make sure she's in one piece when you bring her in. I don't want her mussed up. I aim to treat her right special.'

A flicker of disappointment registered on the mute's face and Orville laughed.

'Don't you worry none. You'll get your reward if you follow orders right. Once I open Wilkins Enterprises I'll need me a fella like you to keep out undesirables.'

A gleeful grin spread over the man's lips and Orville was surprised he didn't do a dance. He had discovered the mute's vulnerability and it was the same as most men's: money.

Orville stared off into the night, pleased with himself. Parker's blundering might have alerted the marshal and Crowly to the fact someone else wanted the mine, but he would turn that to his advantage and take revenge on Grace at the same time.

* ★ ★

The sun rose in a blaze of orange and yellow, glazing Silver Bluff with honey light. Amber jewels sparkled in troughs and glittered from windows and to all intents the street looked as peaceful as it had on any other day.

But it wasn't peaceful, was it? Hell, not by a long shot, and Marshal Jim Morgan had stayed awake half the night dwelling on that fact.

He poised next to the office window, gazing out at the new day and wondering how the hell things had changed so quickly in twenty-four hours. Hadn't he just been lamenting he was stuck in a nowhere town? Now here he was fretting on the fact he'd been forced into killing a man. It left a bitter taste in his mouth, one he hadn't expected, and one that made him realize folks always complained about the things they didn't have. He had foolishly pined for a gal who wanted no part of his world, one who made a fool of him by carrying on with another behind his back and making him the butt of whispered jokes among her haughty contemporaries. He had craved a life of adventure and purpose he figured didn't exist. None of that looked quite so important, now. He had adventure and purpose and it came with a much darker price tag than he expected, the price of a man's life and a threat to a young woman and her uncle. And as for pining over the Lady Wescott? Well, even those feelings grew hazy when he recollected Grace's hand in his last night. Maybe he was just loco, but something about a spitfire of a girl made him realize the Lady Wescott wasn't all he'd built her up to be. Hell, hadn't he known it all along? Most like, but admitting to yourself you'd been taken for a fool was a whole other prospect, wasn't it?

His hand drifted to his arm, fingers kneading the bandage beneath his shirt. The wound was little more than a scratch; it could have been a lot worse.

And that's what he had to think about first, before entertaining thoughts of Grace Crowly in a womanly capacity, which he had little business doing anyway.

Movement across the street caught his attention and his gaze shifted to a woman striding along the boardwalk as if the Devil were on her tail. Grace Crowly, up with the roosters, face saddled with a look that boded ill for anyone foolish enough to get in her way. She had saddle-bags slung over her left shoulder. He wondered what she was up to so early, but reckoned he had better things to attend to than whatever put another burr in her saddle.

He was about to look away when she halted, gazing into the dress-shop window. Her expression softened. The sudden transformation made him all the more inclined to think her attitude was a façade she created to keep folks at a distance. From what the old man had told him about her loss maybe he could understand her ways better, but did it mean anyone could ever break through her defenses? Did he want to try?

The notion of that mule entered his head again and a smile filtered on to his lips. His pa might not have understood what attracted him to that mule, but a boy of twelve had glimpsed something worth salvaging, a gentleness of spirit beneath the surface. That mule had turned into the best friend a loner of a boy ever had.

The young woman moved away from the window and headed towards the livery. He debated going after her, advising her it was best she stayed in her room until he got things figured out, but he bet his chances of convincing her of such without her kicking him way that mule had were about as good as the old man finding a mine in Silver Bluff. So he let her go, against his better judgement, as a man and as a marshal.

Backing away from the window, he went to the coffee-pot, then poured lukewarm Arbuckle's into a tin cup. He swallowed it in three gulps. Hell, Grace was right: he couldn't make coffee that tasted any better than kerosene.

He set the cup down, shaking his head, thoughts returning to last night's events. He had more questions than answers. The prospector had been unable to identify the dead man other than recognizing him from the saloon, which meant someone, perhaps Wilkins, had hired the hardcase. After, Jim spent the remainder of the night sifting through dodgers, finally coming up with a name: Reb Parker. Wanted for a killing in Colorado Springs and likely a dozen other crimes that hadn't made public notice. Whatever the case, Parker was a hired man. Jim was inclined to make a connection to Wilkins but what about the gypsy? Was she involved with the hardcase, or merely acting on her own? Was she after Crowly's mine? Did that mean she took the old man's title seriously, despite the fact the saloon carried the same name? And how had she vanished without him seeing her leave?

Something about her involvement didn't sit well but it was nothing conclusive. One thing he felt certain about: she had made a point of directing Crowly away from Silver Bluff. That was enough in itself to ring warning bells.

He went to the wall rack and plucked his hat from a peg. He would try the saloon first, and if she wasn't there he'd ride on up to their camp. 'Bout time he introduced himself to her husband anyway. He opened the door and stepped out into the new day. With the dissolving chill of the night the air smelled fresh and new, despite the dust and dung stirred by gentle gusts. Downstreet, a horse came from the livery. The woman leading it swung into the saddle and headed east, towards the trail. He again considered trying to stop her but dismissed the notion as quickly as it came. Grace Crowly could take care of herself and would resent any implication to the contrary.

After stopping at the café for a breakfast of bacon, eggs and pan fries, he headed over to the saloon. From what he'd observed in the past, she usually started her day with the birds, which now appeared suspect in itself since most customers wandered into the El Silverado later, except for a few early drunks.

Morning light filtering through grimy windows made the saloon dusky, sepia colored. An old man hunched over a table, head hanging low, glass clenched in his bony fingers. Old Justus, starting the day early, Jim reckoned. His attention shifted to the back. The curtain still hung across the door and the gypsy woman sat at the table, fingers playing over her cards as she laid them out in a crosslike pattern. Her gaze rose to meet his and she gave him a smile he couldn't read. She seemed little concerned over last night's misadventures and he wondered if maybe he hadn't misjudged her. Or was she merely hoping for another consultation with the old man, to discover if her guidance had taken hold?

Jim glanced at the 'keep and the man nodded, face pinched and shades paler than usual. Morgan removed his hat and threaded his way through the tables, the gypsy's gaze unwavering.

'Marshal . . . ' She laid down another card.

He tossed his hat on the table and pulled out a chair, lowering himself on to it. 'Ma'am . . . '

'Have you come for a reading, Marshal? Or perhaps to ask the spirits for guidance?' Her voice was probing, cold, with none of the honey she'd put on at the séance, and he coddled an intense dislike for her. She had the air of a carcass feeder.

'This ain't a business call, Miss Catriona.'

'Oh, no?' She raised a questioning eyebrow but he knew damn well it didn't take a fortune-teller to figure out

148

why he'd come here.

'You hightailed it right quicklike after that shot last night. Where'd you go?'

Her expression didn't change. 'Catriona knows when to make an exit. The spirits were out of alignment.'

'Spare me the act, ma'am. That bullet had my name on it so I ain't inclined to take kindly to any run-around. Fact, I got an empty jail-cell just waitin' to be occupied if you don't feel like answerin' me straight.'

'On what charge, Marshal?' Anger danced in her dark eyes, quickly hidden.

'How 'bout public nakedness for starters?' It was flimsy and he knew it, but the best he could think up at the moment.

She laughed, the sound of it mocking and wholly annoying. 'I was frightened, Marshal. The séance was a draining experience for me and when the shot came I departed.'

'How'd you leave?'

'Why, I walked right out the front.'

His brow cinched. Was she lying? He

couldn't read her on that point. 'How'd you get by without me seeing you?'

'You were occupied with the man you shot, Marshal. It is hardly inconceivable my departure escaped your notice.'

Something in her tone said otherwise, but he let it go. 'Where'd you go?'

'To my husband, Junas.'

'You ain't got a notion why that man might have fired that shot, do you?'

'Why, I have no idea, Marshal. Perhaps the cards could tell us . . . ' Her snake smile was back. He had never cared a lick for snakes, but if he had to make a judgement, he would have said she was telling the truth on that point. It didn't, however, let her off the hook.

'Why'd you tell that old man his silver-mine wasn't here?'

Without missing a beat, she slapped a card down and smiled. 'I did not tell him, Marshal; the spirits did.'

This time she was lying and he knew it, though he reckoned he'd never get her to admit that fact. 'What stake you got in a legendary silver-mine, ma'am?'

'None, Marshal, I assure you. We gypsies lead a simple life and survive on our gifts.'

'And just what might those gifts be?'

'I read the tarots and speak with the dead. My husband performs feats of magic and entertains the weary.'

He reckoned she had other gifts she neglected to mention, such as lying and likely enterprises that involved using her feminine wiles. He'd heard tell she had a couple regulars in town, but enforcing morality wasn't his bailiwick.

'Reckon you're right relaxin' for the weary, too, ma'am.'

Anger jumped back into her dark eyes. 'Just what is that supposed to mean, Marshal?'

'You tell me; you're the fortune-teller.' He let a mocking smile filter on to his face.

She laughed, the expression forced, and placed another card on the table, a peculiar skeleton card that sent a shiver through his being for no reason he could pin-point.

'The death card, Marshal.' Her smile turned colder. 'A most unusual card to reveal at this point, do you not think?'

Although he reckoned he'd seen more originality in dime novels, the card coming up at that point still unnerved him. 'That what it means, death?'

'Perhaps. It certainly means an end. You may be in danger, Marshal. You would do well to heed the advice of the tarot from this point on.'

He uttered an uneasy chuckle and stood, scooping his hat from the table. 'And you might do well to hire a better scripter. In the meantime, you be careful what you tell that old man.'

'I tell only what the spirits reveal, Marshal.'

'I'm sure you do, ma'am.' He set his hat on his head and walked towards the batwings, knowing he had gleaned damn little information. He concluded she had no involvement in the attempt on his life, but was equally convinced she was up to something where Crowly was concerned.

He got halfway across the barroom when the batwings swung inward and the old man walked in. Dark half-moons nested under the prospector's eyes and weariness put a slump in his bony shoulders.

'Mornin', Crowly.' Jim tipped a finger to his hat.

Crowly's nod lacked any energy. 'You seen Grace, Marshal? Thought she might have come here after that gypsy.'

'Saw her earlier, headin' towards the trail. She didn't look none too happy, either, but that seems to be her regular disposition.'

Crowly uttered a thin laugh. 'Don't reckon she was pleased as punch.'

'What bee got under her bonnet this time?'

'We had ourselves a bit of a quarrel.'

'That an unusual occurrence?' Jim offered a sideways smile.

'Ain't unusual at all. Fact, it's far too usual and she does it on purpose.'

'Kind of settled on that conclusion myself. Take it Miss Catriona had something to do with it?'

Crowly nodded, gaze flicking to the gypsy then back to Jim. 'She was right peeled I talked to that gypsy. Said it damn near killed me, getting all worked up that way, and that I was a fool if I believed anything that came out of that woman's mouth.'

'Your niece ain't got the most subtle of deliveries, but her heart's in the right place. And she's right about Catriona. I bet she's right about the séance almost killing you, too. You looked like you had one foot in the grave after that spirit showed up.'

Bowing his head, Crowly looked at the floor for long moments, then back to the marshal. 'Much as I hate to admit it, you're right. Reckon my heart damn near gave out after Millie appeared. I'm too old for this, Marshal. And I'm too old to be searchin' for another mine, even one that ain't forty miles away in Brownville.'

Sympathy for the old man made Jim's throat tighten. Crowly was giving up; that was plain to see. 'Reckon maybe it's time you sat Grace down and had a real talk with her 'bout your heart and your need to make sure she's taken care of. You tell her straight, she just might listen. Arguin' ain't helpin' things any.'

Crowly shook his head. 'She don't want to hear it, Marshal. She's too scared of losing folks she loves, but she won't admit it.'

'You gotta make her hear it. I won't sugarcoat it, Mr Crowly. From the looks of things you best make your peace soon.'

Crowly seemed to deflate even further. 'I won't argue that point, but Grace . . .'

Jim nodded. 'I reckon Grace ain't the easiest woman to talk to but way I see it you got no choice. I figure from what you said her parents left without saying good-bye; don't you do the same. Meantime, let me worry about the silver-mine.'

Crowly's eyes shimmered with tears. 'She needs someone to care enough about her to settle her down, Marshal. I know the right fella could pan the wanderlust out of her blood.'

A sinking sensation hit Jim's belly and heat rushed into his face. He knew what Crowly was gettin' at and he had no desire to follow that trail. 'I'll go find her and send her back, if she'll listen to me. Rest is up to you. Head over to my office and wait for me there.'

Crowly nodded. 'Thanks, Marshal. Guess I got me some thinkin' to do.'

'Reckon you done enough of that already. It's talkin' you best set your sights on.' Jim patted the man's shoulder, then headed out through the batwings. He found himself almost eager to locate Grace, maybe not only for Crowly's sake but for his own selfish reasons. Sometimes a fella just never got tired of gettin' kicked in the head . . .

6

Damn that crazy old fool!

Grace gigged the horse into a gallop and clenched the reins so tightly her hands went bone-white. She cursed Phidias again for listening to a dime-novel fortune-teller and cursed the entire West in general for being so unforgiving of an old man's dreams. She rightly couldn't figure out who she felt so all-fired angry with the most, but suspected it was herself for her inability to control the world around her any better than she had been able to the night her ma and pa died. It had taken her a long time to function at all after that and now everything seemed to be crashing in on her again. God was a horse, in her estimation, one who bloated his belly when you tried to cinch the saddle. He'd let you ride all comfortable-like for a spell then suddenly you'd find yourself hanging upside down or pummeled beneath his galloping hoofs.

You can't blame the Good Lord for your fight with Phid, Grace, she scolded herself. She couldn't blame him for her habit of striking out at the very folks who cared about her most, either.

Could she?

Well, why not? Wasn't God responsible for the bitter young woman who refused to give anyone the chance to get too close so she wouldn't have to face the fact the people you loved most could be snatched from your life without an instant's notice? It was *His* fault. *He* could stop it. *He* could prevent her from being utterly alone and grieving for things that had never been, all because death intervened.

'I hate you!' she shouted with as much fury as she could muster and her heart pounded. 'I hate you all to hell!' Her words of acrimony dissolved in the rush of wind whipping at her body and the clamor of hoof-beats. Yelling at an invisible God was useless and she knew it. Because He never listened. He never granted her a lick of inner peace or comfort. And soon Phid would be gone and laughter would ring out of Heaven, again mocking her pitiful cries for mercy just this once.

Tears welled in her eyes but she quickly forced them away. She reined up, body trembling, and drew shuddering breaths. It took her another five minutes to get the constriction loose from her throat and see the trail ahead clearly enough to heel Ruthie onward.

Guilt washed over her for giving Phid such Jesse this morning. She supposed he wouldn't take it too much to heart; he never did, but the memory of how he looked last night after the séance made her wish she could take back the fight. Sometimes she just couldn't stop herself. Saying she was sorry wasn't one of her strong points, either.

Reaching the side of the stream, she

drew up, letting out a defeated sigh and scanning the surroundings. The notion occurred to her she was placing herself in a vulnerable position after being shot at, but she reckoned she could take care of herself.

She jumped from the saddle and tethered Ruthie to a cottonwood branch. The horse had that spiteful gleam in its eye, so Grace kept alert for any notion the palomino took to bite her in the shoulder. She sometimes wondered why she bothered keeping the jughead, but she reckoned it was because Ruthie was just like her in many ways, a kindred spirit.

'Us gals ain't worth nothin' without a wild side, eh, Ruthie?' she muttered, patting the horse's flank while staring out at the woods. Her gaze shifted to the ridge, then along the trail to make sure no one was spying, but she spotted no signs of a watcher. Maybe after last night whoever was responsible would lie low, thinking the lawdog was on his trail. She doubted the hardcase who fired on the marshal was working alone and she wagered it had something to do with the attempt on her and her uncle, too. Maybe the bullet had even been meant for one of them, instead of the lawman. But who would do such a thing, or hire someone else to do it?

Orville.

The name jumped into her mind and she let out a disgusted *pfft*. Phid might think Orville incapable of such but she knew different. She wouldn't put it past that lunkhead to try anything where money was concerned — or women. She had seen a sickness in that fella's eyes the day he tried to manhandle her person years back and she'd cleaned his clock. Staring up from the ground with his hands clutched firmly to his medicine pouch, he had appeared fully capable of murder. She wagered he hadn't outgrown it.

Sighing, she turned towards the stream, gazing out at the bubbling water. She struggled to cleanse all thoughts of silver-mines and Orville

161

Wilkins from her mind. The sun warmed her back and the breeze felt supple and caressing against her face. With the sensation rose a strange longing. Locking her arms together, she wondered how it would feel to stand here wearing the dress she'd seen in the shop window, the wind shivering its lace and dancing across its frills. How would it feel to step back from all the loss and disappointment and just for a suspended moment allow herself to be a little girl again, wanting the things little girls wanted, dreaming the dreams of a woman? She recollected feeling such things before her parents died, but then choking black smoke poured over those dreams, along with consuming flames that burned away all hope. Phid told her she was lucky to have awoken and climbed out through the cabin window, but she knew luck had nothing to do with it. Fear had driven her, blind panic. At seven she had only thought of herself, instead of going back through the house, trying to wake her parents, save them. Phid assured her later that her folks had no chance and likely smoke had taken them long before she went out the window. Any other move would have doomed her as well. She reckoned he was right but it didn't stop her from feeling responsible somehow.

Tears welled. 'Goddammit,' she mumbled, sniffling. Why had she let her guard down and thought about the dress? Thoughts of hope just brought thoughts of loss. It hurt too much.

What the hell made her think about dresses and hopes, anyway? She had no right to think about herself with Phid feeling so dispirited over not finding that mine. What the goddamn hell was wrong with her? She was usually so good at controlling her emotions, but something was dragging things to the surface.

It was that goddamn marshal, wasn't it? Bastard. With a few kind words about that dress he had made her feel things she had no call feeling. No man had ever called her pretty before, at least not with the sincerity Jim Morgan put on it.

She cursed herself for the feeling of warmth that flooded her innards with the thought.

Hell, what would a man like that want with a dirty saddle tramp like her anyhow? The fella would have to be plumb ass-headed to find any interest in her after the way she had singed his saddle.

She didn't even look like a woman, what with the man's clothing and trail dirt smudged across her face. Christ ridin' a donkey, she stank like a week on the trail and cursed like a drover. Imagine her in a dress anyway! Her, Grace Crowly, damn near as much a gypsy as the fortune-teller in the saloon, and practically an old maid, to boot. Twenty-seven and still in possession of her maidenhood, and likely as not to shoot the first fella who got a notion to take it from her.

She shook her head and wrapped her arms tighter about herself, feeling strangely vulnerable to her memories and even to her desires. For an instant she tried to indulge in the mental image of herself in the dress, but found she could no longer bring it to mind. All she could see was a grimy-faced tomboy, awkward as hell and ugly as a mustache-lipped whore.

Letting her focus return to the stream, she heard the birds twittering in the forest. Was it possible for her to just be a woman and forget everything else in her life: the loss, the death, the future threatening to descend on her like a blue norther? Just for a time?

Unfolding her arms, she plucked her hat from her head and tossed it to the ground. Her fawn-colored hair was pulled tightly back and up and pinned atop her head in a bun. She drew out the pins, letting her locks free to cascade about her shoulders. She fluffed out the tresses, which when washed would be silky though brittle at the ends from years of neglect. Her fingers trembled more than she expected as they went to her dirt-smeared face. She pinched a wad of her blouse and sniffed; her clothes smelled of sweat and old bacon grease. She flinched, almost laughing at the thought of any man wanting her. She couldn't see herself as one of them ladies who soaked their ivory skin in lavender water and preened up like a prize rooster for their menfolk. Hell, she didn't bathe in tubs, she bathed in streams — when she bathed at all.

She surveyed the area a final time to make sure no one was watching, then undid the buttons on her blouse and dropped it to the ground. She kicked off her boots then unbuckled her gunbelt and britches, leaving them in a pile beside her hat and clothing. After, clad only in a red union suit, she stood looking out at the stream, the stray thought she was just washing herself up to look more presentable to that marshal passing through her mind. Maybe she was, but was that so wrong? What harm would it do to at least clean herself up a bit?

Likely none.

She took a breath and shimmied out of her union suit, then walked into the stream. The water was chilly from the previous night and goosebumps sprang out on her arms and breasts. Skin tingling, she lowered herself into the water and splashed her face. It felt invigorating and somehow freeing, as if for an instant she could be that little girl again and let all her burdens float away on the current. She scrubbed the grime from her face until her cheeks were rouged, then sank below the water to soak her hair.

She remained in the water till all the trail dust was scoured from her skin. The sun, climbing higher, warmed the water and sparkled along the surface and glittered from droplets on her flesh. She drew slow soothing breaths of champagne-scented air, relaxing, but the feeling was fleeting. The reality of not finding the mine and her uncle's condition invaded any serenity and womanly notions she might have let herself entertain and the day appeared to turn gloomier. She knew it was only her perception but the mood was shattered and she found herself suddenly unable to tolerate another moment of vulnerability.

She hurriedly stepped from the stream, slapping water from her arms and legs and went to her clothing.

A man came from behind her horse and she let out a startled gasp. She crossed her arms over her breasts, but there wasn't much she could do to hide the fact she was in her birthday suit.

A leering grin welded on to the man's face and she wondered just how long he had been watching her. She didn't recognize the man but his hard features and dull eyes pinned him as a hardcase.

'What the hell you think you're doin', watchin' a gal taking a bath, you sonofabitch?'

The man's grin only widened, infuriating her. If she hadn't been standing in the all-together she would have charged him and kicked that grin off his face.

Her gaze flicked to her clothing and gunbelt. The intent must have shown on her face, because the man made an ugly grunting sound and drew a Smith & Wesson. He thrust it at her, indicating for her to come with him and not try anything stupid.

'Least let me put on my clothes.' Her eyes narrowed and he didn't seem to cotton much to the idea but she went to her clothing anyway, having no desire to be prancing around the woods naked to wherever the hell he intended taking her. He got an eyeful as she hastily pulled on her union suit and buttoned it up. She wasn't particularly shy but something about the way the fella ran his eyes over her body, like a coyote lookin' at a prairie chicken, made her feel ashamed she was a woman at all.

She made a move for her trousers but the man grabbed her arm and yanked her towards the trail. His fingers gouged into her upper arm and she wanted to scratch his eyes out, but checked the urge. She didn't need to antagonize the sonofabitch any further at this point and reckoned a union suit was better than nothing.

Releasing her, the mute went to her horse. He twisted a note under the reins, then walked back to her and jammed the gun into her spine. With a grunt and shove of the barrel, he forced her to climb the hill beside the trail.

* * *

Jim Morgan rode towards the stream, hoping he would be able to persuade Grace Crowly to come back to town without too much trouble. He had his doubts, but this time she would have to listen to reason. Phidias Crowly didn't have much time left and Grace needed to know that.

She needs someone to take care of her . . .

The old man's words nagged at Jim's

mind and while he found the notion more appealing than was comfortable, he might have argued with Crowly that Grace wasn't the type to need anyone taking care of her. Well, maybe that wasn't quite true. Everyone needed someone, didn't they? Even that old mule of his had needed him.

Would Grace need him?

Why does it matter to you, Morgan? Didn't you learn your lesson with Lady Wescott?

But Grace wasn't Lady Wescott. His station in life wouldn't make any difference to her.

What did matter to Grace Crowly?

He found himself at a loss for an answer but reckoned it would prove a hell of a lot different than what mattered to Lady Wescott.

He rode on another half mile, coming from his thoughts as he spotted a horse tied to a cottonwood beside the stream. His gaze scanned the bank in both directions. The area appeared deserted and a sliver of dread pierced him. Would Grace have gone off and left her horse?

Drawing up and dismounting, he looped the reins to a branch. He studied the stream bank, noting footprints in the soft sand at the water's edge. He went to them, knelt. A woman's prints, barefoot; he reckoned Grace had entered the stream at this point. A few feet down were tracks where she'd come out. So where was she now?

The dread increased and he straightened. Eyes alert, he spotted a second set of footprints, these belonging to a man, likely a large one from the indentations they made. They, along with Grace's, led to a hat and pile of clothes a few feet further on. Near the clothes lay a gunbelt he recognized as belonging to the young woman.

'Christ . . . ' he muttered, belly sinking. His gaze skipped along the surrounding woods, but he spotted nothing out of the ordinary and certainly nothing encouraging. Grace Crowly was missing and likely not of her own design.

Dread turned to vague panic laced with reproach at himself for not having tried to stop her earlier. If something fatal had happened to her it would be his fault.

He took a deep breath, struggling to keep himself from dwelling on worst-case conclusions. Gathering up her clothing and wrapping it into a bundle, he went to her horse and stuffed it into her saddle-bags. The horse eyed him with a suspicious glint.

Ice trickled down his spine and he froze as a note twisted in the reins caught his eye. Before he even opened it he knew it held the reason for Grace's disappearance. He plucked it free, his suspicions confirmed the moment he read the contents.

'Christamighty . . . ' he mumbled. His belly churned at the thought of having to tell Crowly about his niece. He prayed it didn't kill the old man.

He shoved the note into his pocket,

then went to his own horse. Untethering the reins, he guided the animal to the trail and slapped the bay's rump. 'Go on home, boy!' The horse bolted. Well trained, it would find its way back to the livery, where the attendant would take care for it for him.

He returned to the palomino, untied it and stepped into the saddle.

Seconds later, he found himself sitting in the stream.

One moment he had been atop the horse and the next, quite unexpectedly, he might add, he found himself airborne, arms windmilling, legs flailing. He landed with a great splash and a subsequent string of curses at the horse and all its kind. He stood, streaming water, and stalked up the bank towards the animal.

'Hell, you got the same goddamn disposition as your owner!' But any anger quickly vanished as he thought about Grace missing. He grabbed the reins. The horse made a nearly successful attempt at biting him in the shoulder but he got out of the way just in time. It was going to be a hell of a ride back to town.

* * *

'Why you all wet?' asked Phidias Crowly as Jim Morgan stepped into his office, water still dripping from his clothing.

'Long story . . . ' Jim's voice carried an edge and the old prospector smiled.

'Didn't try to ride Ruthie, did ya?'

His cheeks heated. He flung his hat on a peg. 'That horse is a menace.'

'Inclined to agree.' Crowly nodded, but worry dawned in his eyes. 'Where's Grace? You wouldn't be ridin' Ruthie if somethin' weren't wrong.'

Jim sighed, looked out into the street for a long moment then back to Crowly. 'Reckon I got some news and it ain't the best. You gotta be strong.'

The old man's legs started to shake visibly and he leaned against the desk for support. 'She . . . ain't dead, is she?'

175

Jim shook his head. 'I reckon she's all right for the moment.'

'Then what happened? She's all I got, Marshal. Please . . . '

Belly sinking, Jim fished the now soggy note, compliments of Ruthie, out of his pocket. 'Someone took her. Must have snuck up on her from the looks of the tracks around the stream.' He passed the note to Crowly and the old man began to tremble uncontrollably as he read it.

'Says if I want her back alive I best find that mine right away and turn over the title.'

'Proves beyond a doubt the motive for shooting at you. Ain't signed but I'm willing to bet your cousin Orville is the most likely suspect.'

'Maybe you're right, Marshal. Looks like his handwritin' and up till last night Orville's the only one who would have known about me searchin' for that mine. But that means Grace's as good as dead because that mine likely don't exist 'cept in my night-mares now . . . '

The old man shuddered, his withered frame seeming as if it would rattle apart. He clutched at his chest and his face washed a shade paler. Jim went to him, gripping the prospector's shoulders.

'You gotta to hold on, Crowly. We might not find that mine but I'll do my damnedest to find Grace and bring her back safe.'

Crowly peered at him, eyes distant for a moment, then the color bled back into his face. 'I believe you will, Marshal, but you got no place to start. Maybe I do.'

Jim let go of the man's shoulders and Crowly straightened, as if he had found new life. Jim's face pinched. Crowly's thoughts were transparent.

'I got a notion what you've got in mind and I don't think it's the best idea.'

'You got another plan right now? I gotta do something, Marshal. Grace's everything to me. I can face going to my Maker but I can't face losing her.'

Jim's voice hardened. 'That gypsy isn't the answer. Last night she was almost the death of you. That's the last thing Grace would want.'

'What choice do I have, Marshal? I sure as hell ain't likely to find that mine and Orville ain't gonna settle for a saloon.'

Jim saw the old man's mind was made up and nodded. Maybe it was best Crowly clung to some small hope, even if it came from a charlatan fortune-teller. 'You do what you think best, Mr Crowly. Meantime I'll ride back out and search the woods. When I get back you let me know what that gypsy says. I don't believe a lick of what she preaches but I want to be there when she does it, at the very least to make sure nothing happens to you.'

Crowly nodded a feeble nod and went to the door, gait shuffling, unsteady. He leaned heavily against the frame, as if the burden of every wrong decision he'd ever made was settling on his shoulders.

'I'll find her, Mr Crowly,' Jim said, knowing it was wrong to promise such a thing but unable to stop himself. Crowly needed hope more than honesty at the moment.

The prospector's eyes shimmered with tears as he looked up. 'Marshal, all the silver in the West don't mean nothin' without my Grace. Forgive an old man his loco indulgences when it comes to that.'

Jim offered a reassuring smile. 'Ain't nothing for me to forgive. Reckon if I were in your place I'd do the same.'

Crowly uttered a forced laugh. 'The hell you would, Marshal, but thanks for showin' an old man respect. Ain't had much of that since Millie passed.'

With that the old man stepped outside and Jim stared after him, praying he could live up to his promise and find Grace Crowly alive.

7

The dusk somehow seemed darker than on previous nights, fraught with menacing shadows and the chill touch of unseen threats. Sitting in the gathering gloom of his office, a wall lantern turned low, Jim Morgan leaned forward in his chair and buried his face in his hands. Frustration and a certain measure of hopelessness cinched in a knot at the back of his neck and a powerful headache commenced. He'd spent the remainder of the day searching for any lead to the whereabouts of Grace Crowly, only to come up empty. Brushed-away tracks and the occasional hoofprint provided little evidence pointing to which direction the kidnapper had taken and he was no Indian sign reader. He couldn't imagine Grace going along peaceable, unable to leave some sort of sign, and he prayed that didn't mean the worst. The more time that passed the less likely became the chances of finding her alive, especially if Crowly didn't come up with that silver-mine.

Did finding the mine really matter as far as Grace's life was concerned? No. Whoever was behind this, Orville Wilkins or some unknown entity, would never turn the young woman loose even after he got what he wanted. The kidnaper wouldn't want the old man around to point the finger, either. Nor some small town marshal. If Orville Wilkins planned on grabbing himself a huge silver-strike, he would do it without witnesses to trouble him later.

He drew his hands away from his face and blew out a frustrated sigh. His nerves cinched and he banged a fist against his desktop. He realized his worry over the young woman's welfare had gone far beyond a lawman's concern, and that it was clouding his thinking. Knowing she was out there, possibly hurt or worse, made every fiber of his being want to add Wilkins to the funeral man's customer list.

Shoving away from the desk, he stood and went to the rack, grabbing his hat. Crowly would be waiting on him at the saloon in a few minutes and he reckoned he had best get over there. Christ, what else could he do without a lead?

'Hell of a lawman you turned out to be,' he muttered to himself, as he stepped out into the cool night. No leads and he was following an old man into a fake fortune-teller's parlor of lies.

The saloon was dark except for a turned-low lantern and the candle flickering on the table. The barkeep came around the counter as Morgan entered. Jim shucked his Stetson and nodded to the man. Crowly hadn't arrived yet but likely would enter momentarily. The gypsy was nowhere in sight.

'Marshal, I gotta tell ya I ain't happy about another spook meetin'.' The 'keep's features welded into worried lines.

'You'll get no argument from me there, but for now we best humor an old man.'

The barman frowned, face pale in the buttery light. 'I've had enough of it, Marshal. This saloon was my life but I ain't inclined to stick around and fight spooks for it.'

Jim might have laughed had the bartender's tone not come with such conviction. 'Ain't no spooks, Jeb. You're talkin' foolishness.'

'How can you say that after last night?' Shock played on the barman's face. 'You heared them. They was clankin' to beat the band and one of 'em even showed up.'

'Ain't convinced they was spooks. Has to be another explanation. Maybe I'll have me another look around your back area come daylight and see if I can't find it.'

'Look all you want but it ain't gonna make any difference.'

'Why's that?' Jim cocked an eyebrow. He didn't care for the resolve filling the 'keep's eyes.

'Gypsy made me an offer for this place and I aim to take her up on it.

Don't want to, but I'm figgerin' on gettin' out while I ain't a spook myself.'

Jim thought about arguing the point, but what good would it do? Talk of spirits and hauntings was plain foolishness, but he saw no way to convince Jeb of that fact. The man's mind was made up.

Something else didn't strike him as foolish, however; a question: what would gypsies want with a saloon? And where would they find the money to buy it? Catriona didn't make enough with her fortune-telling and card-reading to purchase property. Neither did her husband with his magic act, who, far as Jim knew, never came into town. The notion those two were up to no good strengthened a notch.

'Hold off before you do anything rash, Jeb. Give it a few days to see how things play out.'

The 'keep frowned. 'Don't know, Marshal. I'm inclined to just say the hell with it all and get out while I still got my skin.'

'Suit yourself, but this town's got

worse things to worry about than spirits. Best watch your back around the livin' instead of the dead.'

'Ain't sure what you're gettin' at, Marshal.' The bartender peered at him with intent eyes, plainly unconvinced where spirits were concerned.

Jim shrugged. 'Maybe I ain't totally sure, either.' The batwings creaked open behind him and he turned to see Phidias Crowly enter. The old man looked somehow even more slight than he had earlier. Utter defeat showed in his eyes and pinched his weathered face into worried lines. He was a man clutching to a will-o'-the-wisp, and Jim doubted any fortune-teller would change that.

'Evenin', Marshal . . . ' The prospector's gaze locked with Jim's.

Morgan shook his head at the unspoken question in Crowly's eyes: *Did you find my niece?*

The old man nodded, plainly expecting the answer. 'Then I reckon this here's the last chance.'

'I ain't ready to fold my cards yet, Mr

Crowly, but I don't believe Miss Catriona's a chance at all. Reckon tomorrow we'll have you pretend you're lookin' for a mine. Might buy us some time while I search for Grace.'

Crowly's head dropped, then came back up. 'You got feelin's for her, don't you, Marshal?'

Jim wasn't sure whether it was a question or statement, but something inside him felt as uncomfortable as a pair of new boots. 'Just doin' my job.' Was his voice weak? Christ.

Crowly uttered a thin laugh. 'You ain't a good liar, either, Marshal. Your feelin's are plain as day, whether you want to admit them or not.'

The curtains parted and Madam Catriona stepped through, sparing Jim from any further talk about his designs on Grace Crowly and he was thankful for the intrusion. Clad in the velvet gown, the gypsy woman paused, dark eyes surveying the barroom. She nodded to the 'keep, who went to the lantern and extinguished the flame.

Morgan and Crowly moved over to the table, seating themselves, the 'keep coming last. Jim tossed his hat on an empty chair. Catriona let the robe slide from her body but no gasp came from Crowly this time, no sign he even realized her nakedness. One concern occupied his mind and that was Grace.

If Catriona was disappointed in the lack of response she failed to show it. She lowered herself on to the chair and placed her hands on the table.

'No hand-joining tonight?' The question came out more sarcastic than Jim intended but his nerves were tightening by the minute.

'You are an unbeliever, Marshal . . . ' The woman drilled him with her dark eyes. 'Remain quiet or the spirits will not oblige us this evening.'

The reprimand made him feel like a schoolboy slapped with a ruler, but he reckoned any irritation came mostly with himself for not finding a lead to Grace because he didn't give a damn what the gypsy said. He took a notion to tell her which horse she could get on and how far she could ride it, but held his tongue in deference to Crowly.

From beyond the batwings a breeze moaned over the boardwalk and into the room, stirring up sawdust. The candle-flame flickered. The 'keep's face washed a shade paler and Crowly tensed with expectation. Catriona began her wavering, pretending to slip into a trance.

'Phidias Crowly . . . ' Her voice lowered to a husky whisper and she slumped forward, head hanging, mouth open.

'Gracie?' The old man's voice sounded with desperate hope.

'I am here, Uncle Phidias . . . ' The gypsy woman's mouth barely moved. In Jim's estimation her voice didn't sound a lick like Grace's.

'Search for me no longer, Uncle Phidias . . . '

'W-what?' A look of stark terror flashed in the old man's eyes and Jim's belly dropped as he suddenly realized

188

where things were headed. He might have expected the gypsy to tell him Grace had ridden off with some fella; the notion it was going to be a whole hell of a lot worse than that struck him like a winter wind. He decided to put an end to the charade before things went any further but the gypsy woman spoke before he could act.

'I am with the spirits, now, Uncle Phidias . . .'

From behind the curtain a whitish form manifested itself. Anger surged through Jim's veins at the gypsy woman's blatant cruelty. He reckoned the woman had noticed Crowly's spell last night and concluded the old man had a bad heart; she was attempting to send him to his grave, prevent him from challenging her for the saloon.

Jim leaped to his feet, sending his seat scraping backwards across the floor to flip over on to its back in a cloud of sawdust. He started towards the ghostly figure, intending to grab the thing and prove once and for all the gypsy was a fake.

Two things happened before he made it more than a couple steps. Crowly let out a strangled sound and grabbed at his chest. The old man slipped from his chair on to the floor, gasping.

At the same instant, a knife whipped from behind the curtain. If Jim hadn't been moving sideways to get around the table the blade would have buried itself in his face. It flew through the air with a shriek and thudded into another table behind him. He had felt the breeze as it whisked past, nearly shaving off an earlobe.

A flurry of movement came from the curtain. The ghost jerked behind the folds of the drapery. The gypsy woman grabbed her robe and the 'keep bolted for a lantern.

Jim froze, faced with a dilemma. He could go after the knife thrower and possibly catch him before he got away, but if he did, Crowly might die right there on the saloon floor.

'Christ . . . ' he muttered, his humanity getting the better of him. He knelt beside the prospector, lifting the old man's head.

'She . . . she's dead, Marshal . . . ' Crowly uttered, voice breaking. 'It's too late. I got no reason to go on . . . '

Jim glanced at Catriona, who had covered herself and was looking too concerned over the old man's welfare to be sincere. An intense anger flashed across his face for the gypsy woman, but he would see to her later. For now somehow he had to convince the old man it was all an act, that there was still a chance Grace would be found alive.

'She ain't dead, Mr Crowly. I'll find her. You gotta hold on a spell and give me a chance. That gypsy's nothing but a fake. She wants the saloon.'

The old man's eyes became glassy. 'She . . . she . . . '

Christamighty, he was going and damn little Jim could think of saying would keep him in this world if he had lost the will to fight.

'What did she call you, Mr Crowly? I swear I heard her call you Phid.'

'Yes . . . yes, that's right . . . ' His lips barely moved, and Jim could feel his bony frame trembling. Flecks of spittle gathered at the corners of the old man's mouth.

'The gypsy said Uncle Phidias. Grace wouldn't say that, would she?' Jim's heart pounded in his throat and all the heat drained from his hands.

'No, no, she . . . ' Crowly tried to shake his head but failed.

Jim shot the gypsy another glance, the look in his eyes promising that if the old man died she was going to answer for it. The olive-skinned woman's eyes narrowed with hate.

Jim's gaze shifted to the 'keep. 'Get the doc.'

The barman seemed frozen, stricken with shock at the sight of Crowly lying in Jim's arms.

'Now, you sonofabitch!' Jim shouted. The bartender started, then bolted for the doors. The old man gasped and went limp. Jim pressed his fingers to Crowly's throat; the prospector's pulse was thready. 'Christ, hold on, you old bastard.' His voice came out a shaky whisper. Gaze going to the batwings, he prayed the doc would be in time.

★ ★ ★

Catriona could barely control the fury rushing through her veins. How could Junas have risked their operation in such a way? By throwing that knife at a marshal he might have ruined their plans completely. If the old man had not been stricken the way she hoped that lawman might have caught her husband behind the curtain, even with an escape route none in the saloon knew existed.

Bastard!

A scream of rage came from between her clenched teeth as she strode towards his wagon. He was just unlatching the doors and throwing a gauzy white bundle into the back. Closing the doors, he turned just as she reached him. She balled her hand into a fist and swung with all her strength. Her knuckles clacked from his mouth, splitting his lip and bringing a spurt of blood that splattered in a streak across the wagon. His head rocked and anger flashed into his dark eyes.

'Catriona, you are not so smart to do that, uh?' He swiped the blood away with a billowy sleeve and she swore a snarl escaped his lips. He wasn't far from being a goddamn animal sometimes, she thought, and striking him was risky, but fury had overridden her instincts for self-preservation.

'And you are a dumb piece of horse dung, eh, my Junas?' Dark eyes flaming, she spat at his face. Saliva dribbled down his cheek and his eyes narrowed, murder gleaming within them. 'Why did you throw that knife at the lawman? Do you not realize what you have done? You have risked everything!'

'I have risked nothing. He would

have discovered me. I had no choice. He did not see me.'

'You think that matters now? He will come here to question you because there is no one else.'

'Then I will kill him as I did the other marshal.'

She jammed her fists into her hips. She now wore the billowy off-the-shoulder blouse and ragged skirt, having changed from her robe on the way. 'You cannot simply keep killing lawmen, Junas. More will come. We can have this legally. That barkeep's ready to sell.'

'Is he, Catriona? Is he so foolish as to believe your childish performance?'

'Don't they all? I can make a man do anything, Junas. You would be wise to remember that.'

A jealous light dawned in his eyes and she liked it there. She *could* make a man do whatever she wanted and Junas, despite his propensity for violence, was no exception.

'Why has the marshal not followed if

my knife has made him so suspicious, as you say?'

'The old man collapsed, as we hoped. The marshal went with him to the doc's.'

'Then we have nothing to worry over. He will die and the marshal will never know who threw the knife. The barman will sell you the saloon and we will no longer have to hide what we are doing.'

'What about his niece?'

'You said she has vanished. She is dead.'

'What if she isn't? And what about the old bastard's title? Wouldn't do to have that come up if she's not dead. Besides, we don't know who took her. Someone else is involved.'

Junas frowned, dark eyes glinting with confusion and anger. 'I do not like this. Why are so many suddenly interested in this mine, tell me that, my Catriona?'

The same question had nagged her as well. A few days ago no one suspected them of wanting the saloon and her scheme to frighten the 'keep, childish as it appeared, was working the way she wanted it to. Then the old man and his niece had shown up and things had gone, as the locals put it, straight to hell.

'Do not worry, Junas. I will steal the title and things will work the way we planned. The silver will soon be ours free and clear.'

Junas made a scoffing grunt. 'The way you planned, my Catriona. I am merely a traveling gypsy. I have no use for titles. We have enough silver. We should leave now. You are a greedy wench, indeed.'

Before she could stop herself she slapped him full across the face. Blood dripped from his nose and his eyes narrowed to slits. 'I want more, do you not understand that?' she said through clenched teeth. 'I want all of it! I want what gypsies are not allowed. I will have everything life has to offer those pale-faced haughty women in their fancy dresses and rich houses.' Her voice climbed to a shrill pitch.

Junas grabbed her arms and she felt her feet leave the ground as he swung her around and slammed her into the wagon. He jammed his mouth to hers in a harsh kiss that split her lip and brought the gunmetal flavor of blood to her tongue.

Drawing back and squeezing her arms until she winced and let out a mew of pain, Junas's gaze captured hers. 'You want too much, Catriona. Your greed will find us swinging from the white man's rope.'

'You are a fool, Junas. There is so much more to life than we have, than they *allow* us to have. We are no better than animals to them. Why should we not take what is rightfully ours?'

'No, my Catriona, you are the fool. You have enough but you desire more. It will be your undoing and perhaps mine. I do not require so much, no? I am a man of simple pleasures.'

She laughed, a measure of lunacy in her tone. 'You are a man who likes to kill; is that so simple?'

He grinned. 'In my world it is. Do not forget that.' He jammed his lips to hers again and hoisted her skirt.

She took the kiss and bit at his lips, knowing soon, very soon, she too would enjoy the simple pleasure of killing . . .

★ ★ ★

Jim Morgan doubted Phidias Crowly would live out the night. The old man had slipped into a coma and what was holding him to this world was anybody's guess.

A somber mood bracing him as he stepped from the doc's office into the night, he knew he somehow needed to find Grace now more than ever, before her uncle passed. Crowly told him Grace couldn't accept his death, but if she didn't have the chance to say goodbye it would be even harder on her.

That gypsy was going to answer for this. She had deliberately, in his estimation, caused Crowly's heart attack. While he couldn't prove it, he felt certain she wanted the saloon and was willing to kill for it.

Reaching the El Silverado, he pushed through the batwings. He scanned the interior, seeing no sign of her. The 'keep, a solemn look on his face, peered at him from behind the counter.

'She's gone . . . ' The barman grabbed a bottle of whiskey from the hutch and poured himself a shot. He swallowed it in one gulp.

Jim gave a slight nod, half-expecting that would be the case. 'She reckons that'll keep me from her she's got another think comin'.'

He went to the rear table, circling it and pausing before the curtain. He yanked the drape aside, revealing the doorway. He doubted the ghost had left anything behind but it was either occupy himself with a search or go plumb loco worrying about Grace.

Turning back to the barroom, his gaze settled on the chair the woman had used. It was a worn chair, chipped and . . .

Dusty?

A vague notion pricked at his instinct but he wasn't certain what it meant. A coating of that dust lay on the seat. Wasn't unusual for a chair to be dusty in a saloon, but if he recollected right, Catriona hadn't kept anything between herself and the wood. She'd even sat on the chair after donning her robe, which should have cleaned any dust from the surface. Going to the chair, he knelt and ran his fingertips over the dust. In the dim light it appeared an odd bluish color and felt gritty, more like fine sand. He rubbed it between his fingers. Something about the dust . . .

Brow creasing, he stood. He reckoned the dust must have shaken off her robe when she stood. But did that mean anything other than she had walked from her camp and gotten her robe dirty?

The answer eluding him, he stepped through the open door into the back hall. Gaze scrutinizing the floorboards, he searched for more of the dust but the 'keep obviously hadn't cleaned in a spell and the hallway was thick with grime, making finding a specific kind of dust impossible. He reached the back door, intending to have a look at the alley, but when he tried the handle, though it turned the door wouldn't open. He yanked on it; the door wouldn't budge. His gaze traveled along the frame and he discovered the reason: nails had been driven into the wood, sealing the exit.

Surprise crossed his face. The door was nailed shut. So Catriona couldn't have gotten out that way the other night. How had she appeared from behind the curtain, though, and, more important, how had her partner escaped without being seen or, for that matter, gotten in? Jim wasn't ready to start believing in ghosts. There had to be another way.

Turning, he went to the storeroom door and pushed it open. He peered inside, seeing the crates and barrels and wondered just what he was looking for. He stepped into the room and took a closer look but nothing appeared out of place or unusual. Puzzled, he backed out and returned to the barroom.

An unformed suspicion rising in his mind, Morgan stamped on the floor. A solid thud sounded and he stamped on another spot a couple of feet to the left. The same. Disappointment gripped him, though he reckoned he wasn't quite sure what he had hoped to find.

'What the hell you stampin' around for, Marshal?' The 'keep gave him a puzzled look.

'Lookin' for spirits.' It wasn't far from the truth, he figured.

'Find any?' The bartender's expression didn't look hopeful.

'That gypsy go out the back last night or tonight?'

The 'keep shook his head. 'No one goes out the back. Door's been nailed shut since I got here.'

'Why's that?'

'Dunno. Fella who left it to me was more than a mite addled.'

'So you saw her go out the front?'

'Hell, now that you mention it I don't recollect. I was so worried about ghosts I didn't see where she went.'

'What about her partner?'

'What partner?'

'Her husband.'

'Never seen him in here.'

'How's Catriona get in the back?'

The 'keep shrugged. 'Usually she comes in the front way and goes to her table. Before her séance she goes out back there behind the curtain. Said she needs to prepare her mind to receive spirits.'

Jim nodded. 'What about Crowly and his niece, you reckon they noticed how she left the first night?'

'Crowly was sick and his niece was concerned with that. I don't reckon they noticed much of anything, but now that you mention it that gypsy was just sort of gone.'

Sort of gone . . . Another question he

would have to ask Catriona when he found her.

He went to a nearby table and yanked the knife free, the one hurled at him during the séance. Its long blade sported a vicious edge and he wondered whether Catriona's husband, along with his magician tricks, was a knife thrower. He bet he knew the answer.

He shoved the dagger into his gunbelt and glanced back at the 'keep. 'That gypsy comes in tomorrow you tell her to stay put.'

The barman nodded and Jim headed for the batwings. He would go back to the doc's and sit with Crowly for the night. But in the morning he was going to find those gypsies and the spirits weren't the only ones who were going to be talking.

8

Standing at the edge of his camp, arms locked, Orville Wilkins contemplated the girl tied to a lodge-pole pine ten feet away. He'd threaded a bandanna between her teeth and secured it tight behind her head to prevent her from blistering his hide with every un-Christian name she could spew forth; it hadn't stopped her from glaring bloody murder. Ropes bound her ankles and laced her wrists together behind the tree and he right liked the way her full breasts strained against the fabric of the union suit. While eager to enjoy her flesh, he reckoned he was looking forward even more to killing her. It made no difference whether the old man turned over that silver-mine after he found it; Grace Crowly was a dead woman and nothing would deprive him of that delight. Soon after, the old man and that marshal would follow her to the grave.

That marshal worried him, now. The lawdog had scrutinized damn near every inch of the woods looking for Grace Crowly. At one point, the mute had been forced to knock Grace over the head after she started to kick up a fuss when she got wind the lawman was close to their camp. For a few tense moments Orville had feared the hard-case had hit her too hard and robbed him of his revenge, but she had revived two hours later, likely with a powerful headache and certainly with no improvement in her disposition. Orville wondered whether he shouldn't have taken care of the marshal right there and then, but the lawdog had been ready for trouble; Orville preferred to catch his victims by surprise and save any risk to his own hide. He cursed Reb Parker for making killing a lawman necessary. The stupid bastard. If he hadn't fired at Crowly in the first place, the old man and his niece would have simply vanished after they led him to the mine, with no one the wiser.

He glanced at the mute, who stood a few feet away, smoking a hand-rolled cigarette. There was his huckleberry where the marshal was concerned. Unlocking his arms, he went to the hardcase, who looked up, no expression on his features.

Orville kept his voice low and nodded in the direction of town. 'That lawman . . . you go keep an eye out for him at the edge of the trail. He comes up here again don't waste any time burying him. Don't come back for a spell, either. I aim to spend a little time with our guest, you savvy?'

The mute grinned and tossed his cigarette to the ground. He headed through the woods towards the trail.

Orville peered at Grace Crowly and a lascivious glint played in his eyes. He removed his derby and hung it on a branch. As he moved towards her, Grace's green eyes narrowed with malice and he almost laughed. Christ, he sure was going to enjoy exchanging that expression for one of fear and humiliation. He recollected the time years back when she spurned his advances and vicious desire careened through his blood. She owed him for what she had done, and it was about time she started paying her debt.

★   ★   ★

Grace swore a mule was stomping around inside her skull. Bursts of blinding pain occasionally made her vision blurry, despite the fact nearly half a day had passed since the mute pistol-whipped her. She was lucky the blow hadn't scrambled her brains. She shivered with the thought, a moment of fear overpowering the fury burning in her innards. An instant later, the rage swept back in, all of it directed at the lousy sonofabitch standing ten feet away. The rage mixed with a goodly measure of humiliation at constantly being leered at by Orville and his freak of a henchman. When she got loose she would kick Orville's teeth all the way to Denver. But getting loose was the problem.

She had worked carefully throughout the night, sliding the ropes against the back of the tree, scraping them against the rough bark until strands began to fray. It was a tedious process and she'd damn near rubbed half the flesh off the insides of her wrists. The open wounds stung like hell and the fibers bit into the tender flesh. At times she had to bite down hard on the bandanna to stop tears from streaming, betraying her actions. Just a few moments ago she'd given the bonds a sharp tug and felt them slacken a fraction as fibers parted. A glimmer of hope told her she was close to freeing herself. But she needed a few more minutes and from the look on Orville's face it wouldn't be long before he did more than stare.

Redoubling her efforts, fighting to ignore the agony radiating through her hands and forearms, she worked the ropes against the bark with renewed urgency. It was a struggle to prevent any expression of pain from showing on her face.

She froze suddenly as Orville cast her a glance, then moved towards the mute. Her cousin said something to the hardcase she couldn't hear and the man moved off, disappearing into the forest.

Orville raked her with another of those prolonged accountin's of her womanly charms and her innards clutched with disgust.

He sauntered over to her — she supposed he thought he was being manly but the swagger was as impotent as a skunk with no stink. Getting down on one knee, he peered at her face and her heart started to pound.

He grinned, obviously quite pleased with himself over what he had in mind. 'I take out the gag you promise not to scream?'

What the hell, she thought, nodding. The damn thing was biting into the sides of her mouth and it was unlikely anyone would hear her cries out here anyway.

Orville yanked the gag free and she spat at him. Hell, she hadn't promised not to spit, had she?

Saliva dripped down his face and crimson flooded his cheeks. The back of his hand flashed up in a crisp arc, taking her full across the mouth. Her head rocked under the impact and she stifled a bleat. Blood snaked from her lip and pain shivered through her teeth.

But any discomfort caused by the blow became secondary to the surge of relief that suddenly filled her being. With Orville's blow she had jerked hard on the back of her hands and an abrupt loosening of pressure told her the ropes had snapped. She kept her hands behind the tree, making sure Orville didn't realize what had happened.

'You ain't got any nicer since we were young'ns, Grace.' With a forearm, he swiped the saliva from his cheek.

She peered at him with a look of disgust. 'Might say the same for you,

you lowly sonofabitch.'

The crimson in Orville's cheeks deepened to purple, but he didn't hit her this time. She was thankful for that. Her head and face ached to high hell as it was and another blow might reveal she was no longer tied.

Orville reached out, grasping strands of her hair, letting them drift through his fingers. 'You don't have to die, Grace . . . '

Revulsion raised bile in her throat. 'What makes you think I'd believe a word you say?'

He ignored her, a glassy look of wantonness in his gaze. His fingers brushed her cheek. 'You look right pretty when you ain't all dressed up like a fella.' His hand drifted downward and a chill slithered along her spine.

'You best recollect what happened the last time you tried that.' The venom in her voice made his hand stop, withdraw, but she knew it was only a temporary reprieve.

'You'd be a hell of a lot better off

being nice to me, Grace. You might even like it.'

'Go to hell, Orville, and take your mute and the gypsies with you.'

Puzzlement flickered across Orville's features. She wondered why but wasted no time trying to figure it out. Behind the pine, her hand eased to the ground, fingers probing for anything she could use as a weapon.

Orville's face darkened and his eyes narrowed. 'What the hell you mean about takin' those gypsies with me?'

So that was it. The gypsies weren't working with Orville. They were scheming on their own, but that was the least of her worries for the moment. It gave her an idea, however. If she could distract Orville long enough to get her hands on something solid . . .

'Ain't they workin' with you?' She forced her voice to sound as sincere as she could manage while her fingers explored the ground at the base of the pine.

Orville shook his head. 'Mute's the

only one workin' with me. Other fella I hired met with an unfortunate accident in town.'

She uttered a thin laugh. 'Well, hell's bells, Orville, you best find that mine fast because you got competition.'

The expression of shock that swept over his face was almost ludicrous. 'Who are they?'

'Gypsy fortune-teller at the saloon and her husband. Got themselves a camp at the edge of town . . . ' There! Something pitted, solid, roughly four inches around was wedged into the soil at the base of the tree. A rock, one just the right size to brain Orville with if she could only work it loose.

'They're after the mine?' His tone went cold. She could tell he was not at all pleased with the prospect of others involved.

She tried to make her voice cheerful, goading. 'Reckon so. She told Phid to go search for it in Brownville after he showed her the title. Said the mine wasn't 'round these parts. She must

215

want it all to herself.'

The creases in Orville's brow became gullies. 'Hell, that don't make sense. What would gypsies care about a mine?'

'Don't make sense to me, neither, Orville. Maybe you best have a parley with them and find out.'

'Reckon I intend to. Ain't no reason gypsies would be interested in some old man's claim unless . . . ' He let the words trail off and she wondered what he was thinking. It suddenly didn't matter. The rock came loose. Her fingers curled around it. Now she had to get him to lean in. If she could stun him long enough to grab the knife at his waist and cut her ankles free . . .

'Forget about them gypsies, Orville. You got me to think about instead.' Nausea rose even as she said it but she needed his attention focused on her now.

The lascivious light jumped back into Orville's eyes. His hand groped at her breast and she choked back a sound of disgust.

'Maybe you should try kissin' me, Orville. I might like it.' She said it with all the sincerity she could muster, but didn't quite pull it off. A suspicious look dawned in his eyes and understanding flashed across his features an instant later.

She had no choice but to make her move. If she didn't act she'd forfeit any chance of escape. She whipped her arm from behind the tree. Muscles aching from being tied for so long, movement was awkward and stiff. Throwing her weight forward, she swung the rock, unable to put much force into the blow.

Orville endeavored to scramble backwards but she got lucky. The stone glanced from his temple, stunning him. He fell back, groaning. Momentum brought her forward on top of him and she struggled to position herself for a follow-up blow. Her arms refused to work right, waves of vicious tingles sweeping from her shoulders to her fingertips. Her entire body felt stiff, uncoordinated, but she managed to hoist the stone above his face before he recovered completely.

Even so, he grabbed her wrist and dug his nails into the raw flesh, which sent bolts of excruciating pain radiating through her arm. She let out a gasp and dropped the stone.

He tried to twist her around, get on top of her. She jack-knifed her legs and a satisfying *woosh* of air exploded from his lungs as her knees connected with his crotch.

Orville lost all interest in anything other than clutching his southern borders. He rolled off her and lay groaning.

'Told you you'd get the same thing, you sonofabitch!' She dropped the rock and then snatched the knife from the sheath at his waist. After slicing through the bonds, she hurled the knife aside, and pushed herself to her hands and knees. Struggling to her feet, legs wobbly, weak, she staggered into the woods.

Orville was floundering, kicking up

clumps of soil in an effort to regain his feet and give chase. Gurgling noises came from his mouth as he tried to yell.

With each step the circulation flowed into her legs. Heading in a direction opposite from the one the mute had taken, she ran with everything she had until her muscles quivered with exhaustion and breath burned in her lungs. She tripped over an exposed root and slammed into the ground. Branches tore a swatch from the arm of her union suit, drawing blood. She got to her feet again, panting, heart pounding, and didn't stop running until she reached town.

* * *

The front door to the doctor's office burst open and Jim Morgan turned from where he was gently closing the door to the back room. Shock, then relief flashed across his face as Grace Crowly, dressed in a ragged red union suit, ran towards him.

'Where's Phid?' she demanded and he got in front of her, grabbing her shoulders.

His face went serious. 'Just hold on a minute, Grace. We best talk before you go in there.'

Her eyes narrowed as she jerked from his grip. 'Saloon man told me Phid was here. Said he collapsed last night after talkin' to that gypsy.'

The doctor, an older man with muttonchop sideburns and a grim look on his face, peered at the girl. 'You the niece the marshal told me about?'

She nodded, but kept her gaze locked on Jim and he felt his heart clutch. 'Marshal, Orville's the one who kidnapped me, him and some freak hardcase he's got working with him. I got loose and brained him. You might still catch him off the trail in the woods, due west a half-mile.

Jim frowned. 'I'll get him, Miss Crowly, but right now you best brace yourself.'

'What happened to him? He's alive,

ain't he? Tell me he's alive . . . please . . . '
Her voice trailed off, breaking. She was
starting to come apart and Jim Morgan
suddenly felt awkward and unsure about
what to say or do next.

'I'm powerful sorry, Grace . . . Doc
did the best he could.'

'No . . . ' Her voice became weak and
she stared at him with pleading eyes
that begged him to tell her Phidias
Crowly was alive and coming through
that door at any moment. The honest
pain in her eyes tore something up
inside him, made his throat constrict
with emotion and his heart bleed. He
couldn't recollect ever having felt so
utterly helpless, because no matter how
much he wanted to tell her different he
couldn't change the fact that Phidias
Crowly had died ten minutes before she
came through the door.

Grace suddenly flung herself at him,
balling her fists and beating on his
chest. He stood there, taking it, until
she'd spent her fury.

'Nooo . . . ' she muttered over and

over and suddenly he gathered her in his arms and she stopped struggling, sobbing into his shoulder. He didn't move, didn't speak, and he wished to hell he was better with words than he was.

She pushed away from him, keeping her face turned so he wouldn't see her tears, then ran to the door leading to the back room. All the strength seemed to drain out of her as she reached it, and she leaned heavily against the frame.

'Grace . . . ' Jim whispered.

'Yeah . . . ?' Her voice fluttered, heavy with sorrow.

'I'm sorry . . . I truly am.'

She gave a jerky nod and, hand trembling as she turned the glass knob, opened the door. Jim watched her take tentative steps, stopping as her gaze settled on the thin blanket-covered body lying on the bed. She closed the door on them and Jim glanced at the doctor, who shook his head.

'Ain't never easy, facing the death of

a loved one . . . '

A grim expression welded on to his face. 'Reckon it ain't. She comes out tell her I'm going after the men who kidnapped her.'

The sawbones nodded. 'She's been through a hell of a lot, hasn't she?'

Jim frowned. 'More than her share. I'm gonna see to it someone pays for that.'

9

A few hundred yards down the trail Jim Morgan reined up and dismounted. He tethered the bay to a branch and surveyed the area, keeping an alert eye for any sign of Orville Wilkins and the man Grace said was working for him. He couldn't bring Phidias Crowly back but could do something about the men seeking to steal the silver-mine. After that, he'd deal with the gypsies for their part in hastening the old man's demise.

He went forward, skirting the edge of the trail and searching for any sign of the men. The sun glared high overhead, rays arcing through the branches in glowing shafts. Weird fluttering shadows cast from boughs made the woodland appear somehow threatening. Sweat trickled down his back and his heart stepped up a beat. The feeling of someone watching him returned, stronger this time, yet he spotted no one.

Wilkins's camp had to be nearby. Jim must have nearly stumbled over it yesterday and perhaps Wilkins's man had been observing him the whole time.

Jim started up the rise, ready to go for his gun at the slightest excuse. The impression of being observed intensified, crawling through his nerves like fire ants. Still he saw no one. Enough time had passed, roughly a half-hour from when Grace escaped until now, for Wilkins to have pulled stakes, but Morgan doubted the man would go far. He'd gone to too much trouble to simply ride off.

A sudden movement came from his right, a flash of clothing, as an arm swept up from behind a man-high clump of brush and sunlight glinted off metal. Instinct taking over, he dove forward just as a shot thundered through the morning silence. Lead plowed into a spruce a fraction of an inch from where he had stood an instant before. The bullet narrowly missed taking off his head.

He hit the ground and rolled, coming to his feet behind a thick cottonwood. A second shot chipped bark and splinters from the tree entirely too close to his face. His hand swept to his Peacemaker, freeing the weapon from its holster and bringing it up in front of his chest. Blood pounded in his ears and throbbed in his temples.

Twenty feet to the left, a large man sprang from the brush and darted for the cover of a boulder. Morgan jerked a shot, taking hasty aim on the streaking target, missing.

The man, upon reaching the boulder, promptly triggered another shot but this one went far wide, the bullet burying itself in the ground.

He took a chance then. With the bushwhacker entrenched, Jim could hope for no more than a standoff if he didn't draw out his quarry. The trick was not presenting too big a target.

He spotted a large lodgepole about

thirty feet to the right, near the edge of the trail. Giving himself no time to back out, he bolted for the pine. Twisting his body, he blasted covering shots as he ran.

The bushwhacker popped up from behind the boulder and tried to draw a bead on Jim's moving form. The hardcase fired — once, twice, three times. Lead stitched a line behind his heels, nearly picking him off.

Jim reached the tree unscathed, this one thicker, offering more protection. His breath beat out in hot gasps and his lungs ached. His heart pounded.

A noise. Something crashing through brush. He looked up to see the man swerving towards him. Shock tightened his face. The bastard was taking a huge chance, wasn't he? Why the hell —

'Christamighty!' Jim whispered, truth suddenly dawning on him. Knowing the move was useless, he raised his gun and fired. Even before the hammer fell with an empty clack he knew he had already fired all six bullets. The hardcase knew it, too, and was seizing the advantage.

Jim cursed himself for not thinking out his move better. With frantic fingers he popped the gate on his gun, then pried bullets from his belt, but he was out of time. The hardcase jerked up his own gun and aimed straight at Jim's chest.

The mute grinned, squeezed the trigger. Jim flinched, bracing himself for the burning punch of lead that would come within the next instant.

A hollow clack sounded.

Morgan almost let out a laugh of relief. The man had been too busy counting his adversary's shots to pay attention to his own. He had emptied his chambers.

'Bet it ain't half as goddamn funny now,' he blurted and hurled himself at the man. The killer recovered from his surprise and flung his gun at Jim. Morgan ducked. Although the gun flew past his shoulder he couldn't right himself fast enough to avoid a blow from the man's blocky fist. The punch caught him on the chin and sent himself stumbling backward. Stars exploded before his eyes and for an instant he wasn't sure whether he was standing or falling or even conscious.

He shook his head, fighting a case of the spins. Somehow he had managed to keep on his feet, but it likely wouldn't do him a damn bit of good. His attacker grabbed for the Bowie knife at his waist and whisked it free. He slashed at the air, viciousness in his eyes.

Jim got a bit of luck. The man wasn't skilled with handling a knife; he chopped straight down as he lunged.

Morgan side-stepped, snapping a fist into the man's side. A satisfying crack sounded as a rib fractured, but the man barely seemed to notice.

The attacker twisted, taking a back-handed swipe with the Bowie. Jim ducked under the swing then snapped upright, looping an uppercut. The blow cracked from the man's chin, snapping his teeth together. The attacker staggered but held his feet.

Jim stepped in, planning to allow his antagonist no chance to recover. Although lumbering, the hardcase was far stronger and if Morgan didn't finish him off fast he wouldn't get a second chance.

With a strangled roar, the mute twisted, jerking the Bowie, which he had managed to hold on to, high over his head for another chopping blow. The move caught Jim flat-footed, stopping him in his tracks, and he had one chance to halt the blade from cleaving through his shoulder.

He thrust both arms upwards, hands open, catching the man's descending wrist. In the same move, using the hardcase's own momentum, he swept the blow down and around. With a grisly crunching sound, the knife embedded itself in the man's solar plexus.

The attacker gasped and blood blew in a spray from his mouth. He collapsed, hitting the ground with a thud, then lay still. The blade had likely pierced his heart and he had died in his tracks.

Lying on the ground, Orville Wilkins spat and gingerly felt the livid egg swelling at his temple. The bump hurt like hell and bothered him only slightly more than the ball of nausea twisting in his belly resulting from the knees Grace Crowly had buried in his groin. Again. Christ, that bitch would pay for that — with her life.

Right after he got the silver-mine.

For he reckoned she had provided him with a sure clue to its whereabouts, though she didn't rightly know it. Why would gypsies be interested in sending the old man away from Silver Bluff? Perhaps because they had something they didn't want to give back?

He was willing to bet on it.

Orville gained his feet, sweat pouring from his forehead, head swimming. He sucked deep breaths until another burst of nausea subsided, then grabbed his derby from the branch. Grace would run right to that lawdog and send him

231

back here, but Orville would be long gone by then. Let the mute deal with the tin star.

In the meantime, he would find that gypsy camp and make sure they realized just who owned that silver-mine: Orville Wilkins. And he wasn't about to share.

★   ★   ★

Jim Morgan walked along the board-walk towards Mrs Philbert's boarding-house after searching the woods for any sign of Orville Wilkins. He'd discovered two horses tethered to trees along with evidence of a camp, but little else. Wilkins had either hidden himself or lit off somewhere on foot.

Every muscle in his body ached from his fight with the mute. He had been lucky to survive with only paining limbs. On his way back to town, Morgan had made two stops, the first to see to it the funeral man removed the mute's body from the trailside and the second to retrieve the bundle wrapped in brown paper, now tucked beneath his arm.

The walk and search for Crowly's renegade cousin had provided him with plenty of time to think about Grace Crowly and silver-mines, about Orville Wilkins and gypsies. Most of the conclusions he had reached were based on slim evidence and conjecture and now remained to be proven, but he wagered they were close to the truth. Those gypsies had another way into and out of that saloon; he only had to find it. He felt certain they were working separately from Wilkins, and reckoned he had figured out why, though he would keep it from Grace for the time being. False hope was the last thing she needed. First he'd pay Catriona's husband a visit and confirm his theory.

Reaching the boarding-house, he opened the door and stepped into a small entryway. Before him rose a stairway that led up to a landing with a round stained-glass window.

He climbed the stairs to Grace Crowly's room — Mrs Philbert only rented one room and it was rarely occupied — and knocked gently on the panel. His heart stepped up a beat at the prospect of facing the young woman again, but at the same time he needed to see her, wanted to know she was all right and comfort her if he could.

She opened the door and quickly looked away. The redness in her eyes and dark pouches beneath told him she had been crying.

'It's gone, Marshal . . . ' Her voice wavered, heavy with grief. She had dressed in the clothing he'd retrieved from the stream bank but had left her hair loose over her shoulders and wore no hat. Her lips were swollen and she had a lump on the side of her jaw, compliments, he reckoned, of Orville Wilkins. Despite that, he reckoned she was the prettiest thing he'd ever laid eyes on.

'What's gone?'

'The title. Phid left it tucked in his saddle-bags. He didn't want to take it with him to the séance so he left it in the room but someone broke in and took it. I found the window up and some personals of his scattered on the floor.'

Jim sighed. 'Reckon Orville ain't likely responsible for that. I didn't find him but I found his man and I doubt your cousin had time to sneak into town so quick.'

She nodded, keeping her face turned from him. 'Who then?'

'I'd wager it was one of the gypsies. I'm going to take a ride out to their camp and see if I can't get some answers out of Catriona's husband. You stay here and don't open the door to any one but me in case Orville comes lookin' for you.'

Another nod but he wasn't convinced she had heard what he said. He looked at the floor and tried to think of something to say that might ease her loss, but the words escaped him.

Instead he went to her and handed her the paper-wrapped bundle. Unable to look him directly in the eye, she accepted it and backed toward the bed, sitting heavily on the edge as if all the strength had deserted her, the bundle in her lap. When she finally lifted her head, he saw tears streaming from her eyes. He reckoned it had taken a lot for her to show him those tears.

'What . . . what is it . . . ?' The words came out a whisper.

He shifted feet and his mouth felt full of cotton. 'Somethin' you were admiring. I know it won't do a lick to ease the pain you're feeling but I hope it will tell you you ain't alone. I ain't a particularly sentimental man; never had the chance to be. But you bring out some feelin's in me I ain't never felt. I know it ain't the time to even tell you, considering all you been through, and rightly I don't know why I am. Maybe I just want you to know you don't have to bear your pain by yourself. Let's just leave it at that for now.'

She nodded, more tears rushing from her eyes and dripping on to the brown wrapper.

He backed from the room, gently closing the door behind him. He wondered if the West held any justice for a woman like Grace Crowly, any peace, and he wondered if he could give it to her.

* * *

Grace Crowly stared at the door after it was closed and wanted with all her being to shout at Jim Morgan to stay and hold her. But she couldn't. She had never asked a man for that and with the pain and grief and confusion rushing through her body she didn't know whether she should ask for it now or simply deny the fact she was utterly alone and needed someone.

Phid was gone. Nothing would change that and refusing to accept it would do no good. Not now. Not ever. And the damnable thing about it was she had known he was dying all along. She had seen it in his eyes, seen the times his face had gone pale and he'd tried to hide some kind of pain gripping his chest. She hadn't asked because she hadn't dared hear the answer.

'You stubborn fool!' she yelled at herself, wishing she could go back in time and say she loved him, say goodbye. She had spent an hour holding his cold hand at the doc's and gruffly brushed aside any sympathy the sawbones tried to extend. She didn't want his sympathy, but she wanted Jim Morgan's. Yet she simply did not know how to ask for it or accept it when it was offered.

She sniffled and her hands drifted over the top of the package, more tears dripping on to the wrapping. With trembling fingers she pulled away a corner of the paper, and blue material showed through. A small gasp escaped her lips as she tore the rest of the wrapping away and pulled out the dress she had been admiring in the shop window. Renewed sorrow shuddered through her body because her uncle would never see her wear it.

Phid was gone. Forever. She had no choice but to face that fact. She was alone and there was no silver-mine.

A surge of anger overwhelming her, she flung the dress aside on the bed. No silver-mine, but there was a title and it was gone, too. She could damn well make someone answer for that and it would help ease her pain, her emptiness.

The gypsies, the marshal said. They had stolen it. And she could blame Catriona for hastening Phid's death as well. Those gypsies wanted his mine. The marshal said he was riding out to their camp, but the dark-haired woman might well be at the saloon.

She stood, steeling herself, and wiped the tears from her face. Fingers curling in a tight grip around the butt of the Peacemaker at her hip, a humorless laugh escaped her lips.

She bet that gypsy fortune-teller wouldn't predict what was coming . . .

10

Orville Wilkins made his way around the first of the two wooden wagons at the gypsy camp, gun in hand, caution in his step. Glancing at the legends on each, he scoffed. Fortune-tellers and magic; a load of flop. Only magic in this world involved cold hard cash. And silver. But he hadn't come here to have his fortune told, for he already knew his destiny and it came with the name Wilkins Enterprises. No, he had come because he reckoned those gypsies had something he wanted. Somehow those gypsies had stumbled on to the silver-mine, if he read Grace's words correctly. And they were endeavoring to keep it to themselves. A pity they wouldn't remain alive long enough to reap the rewards of their efforts, but Orville had gone to far too much trouble to let them succeed and he wasn't in the market for partners.

Gaze sweeping over the camp, he spotted no signs of life. Where the hell had those gypsies gotten off to? Perhaps the woman was at the saloon, but what about the husband? Where was he?

He went to the first wagon, the one sporting the man's name. Easing open the left back door, he kept his gun ready in case the gypsy was inside. The wagon was empty of humanity but what he saw brought a smile to his lips.

The interior held a bench cluttered with various tools for pulverizing rock. Molds and a bundle of dynamite rested next to a dish of mercury, which, from what little he knew about silver-mining, was used for amalgamation. The mercury collected particles of silver and gold, which melted within the element, from ground ore. The particles were then filtered out using heat. Gaze moving on, he spotted chunks of quartz and plates of heavy blue sand. He grinned. So the old man's mine was more than a legend after all. Crowly would do a dance if he saw this little operation, but then the old man and his niece were too stupid to figure it out. So was the marshal. Imagine being outsmarted by a couple of gypsies.

At the end of the table a wad of gauze and a sheet of thin material covering a rubber bladder were thrown into a pile. A prop for séances, no doubt, but such theatrics were none of his concern.

A sound caught his attention and he eased around the wagon just in time to see a large patch of brush at the base of the bluff rustling aside. A man came from within the brush and Orville reckoned he had just hit the mother lode. A coating of grime and sweat covered the fellow, a gypsy, who stopped abruptly as he noticed Orville aiming a gun at his chest.

A cold smile spread across Orville's lips. 'Why, thank you, my good man. You have just saved me a hell of a lot of trouble. Here's your reward.'

With that, he pulled the trigger and blasted a hole in the gypsy's forehead.

★ ★ ★

As he approached the gypsy camp, Jim Morgan slowed his bay. If he guessed right Grace Crowly would own her silver-mine very soon. He should have figured it out earlier but he had presumed the mine to be only rumor, dime-novel fodder. He hadn't considered it might actually exist, but it was the only explanation that made sense of Catriona's actions.

The gypsies had found the mine. And somehow it connected with the way they came and went from the saloon without being seen — and with their attempt to frighten the 'keep into selling. If his theory was right, the silver-mine somehow led directly beneath the saloon. That would explain the dust in Catriona's chair and the mysterious clanking heard by the bartender. The dust wasn't plain dust; it was silver dust, clinging, heavy and grayish. That's why they wanted the watering-hole, to claim what lay beneath. Problem was, they hadn't reckoned on Crowly showing up with the title.

He drew up as he reached the camp, keeping an eye out for any sign of the gypsy's husband. The place appeared deserted and a vague dread settled in his belly. Catriona might have returned to the saloon; she probably felt confident he had no concrete charges on which to arrest her and she was right. For now. But the husband should have been here.

Dismounting, Jim drew his Peacemaker as the dread stepped up a notch. The wind stirred up twisting snakes of dust and scratched against the sides of the wagons. Something set off warning bells in his mind, but he had no idea what made him feel that way. Everything looked peaceful enough, just deserted.

Shrugging off the feeling, he made

his way to the first wagon. A door hung open; a gust banged it against the wagon side as he eased up and peered within, fingers tightening on his Colt.

The interior was empty, but what he saw resting on a bench confirmed his suspicions about the gypsies. The mine was indeed real and they had found it. From all indications, they were working the silver, excavating ore in modest amounts. Likely had they kept at it they would have built themselves a sizable fortune with no one ever the wiser. Apparently they had gotten greedy and conspired to steal total ownership.

His gaze lingered on the gauzy material covering a rubber bladder. A hollow tube was attached to one end, for blowing up the balloon, which had a vaguely human, if deflated, shape. He frowned. Lying in a pile was the explanation for the fake ghost that sent Phidias Crowly to his final reward.

Backing away from the wagon, he went to the second conveyance and opened the back doors. This cart revealed racks of hanging gypsy clothing and an old mattress, but little else.

Coming around the wagon he paused, debating his next move. Where had the husband gone to? Was he in the mine? If the mine ran beneath the saloon, there had to be another opening. But where? He wagered it would be close by or they wouldn't have set up camp on this spot; they would have staked out closer to the stream. It occurred to him the former marshal had met with his accident in this area and Jim wondered if the death and those gypsies were connected.

His gaze jumped to the bluff twenty yards away. The sides were studded with scrub pine and man-high brush clumped at its base. The rock above the brush sparkled with captured sunlight, indicating the presence of either mica or feldspar, and quartz. Silver was commonly found in quartz.

He went to the brush, with a sweep of his arm thrusting it aside. A small sound of amazement escaped his lips. Behind the brush was an opening roughly five feet high and five wide. It bore right into the rock wall and a flaxen glow came from within.

A sound made him stiffen, a slight scuffing noise, and he cast a backward glance, wondering if it had been his horse shifting feet. While he glimpsed nothing suspicious, he couldn't stop another chill from slithering down his back.

Gripping his nerves, he swept the brush aside. Bending low, he entered the opening. The shaft within was higher, wider, roughly ten feet wide, with a vaulted ceiling. Heavy beams and supports, spaced at roughly fifty-foot intervals, ran along a tunnel that burrowed deep into the earth.

A sinking sensation hit his belly and his gaze came to an abrupt halt. Twenty feet ahead lay a body. Buttery light from a wall lantern made the sprawled form appear somehow unearthly. Swallowing hard, he went to the man and knelt. Rolling the body on to its back, he saw an ugly bloodless hole in the man's forehead.

He no longer needed to search for Catriona's husband; he'd found him, but someone else had found him first.

'Wilkins . . . ' The name came from his lips just as an explosion rocked the tunnel. The force of the blast kicked him like a thousand-pound mule and sent him bounding forward a good ten feet to hit the ground on his belly. For a moment he wasn't certain whether he lost consciousness, because an instant later he was propped against the side of the tunnel and his gun lay in the dirt ten feet away. Thunder echoed in his ears and every bone in his body pained. A trickle of blood wandered from his mouth.

The first lantern had blown out but fuzzy golden light told him there were more lamps further down the tunnel. A thick cloud of dust coated his clothing. He struggled to his feet, legs wobbly as he took tentative steps towards the mouth of the tunnel, which had become no more than a dark mound of rock and swirling dust. A laugh sounded from beyond the rubble.

'Congratulations, Marshal. You ain't as stupid as I reckoned.'

'Wilkins?' Jim's shout seemed to hang in the air, muffled and reverberative.

'Ah, I see the old man has been talking . . . '

'You sealed off the mine, Wilkins. How you expect to get the silver out now?' He knew the question was foolish even as he said it but his head was spinning and the realization he was trapped in the shaft cut through him like an icy wind.

'I don't have to, Marshal. By the time I take care of some loose ends and hire the proper crews you'll have long suffocated or starved.'

'They'll find bodies and one will have a hole in his forehead, Wilkins. That won't be so easy to explain away.'

'Won't matter, Marshal. I know the right people. I'll hire men who'll keep their mouths shut.'

Loose ends. The words shuddered through his mind and he knew Orville meant Grace and the gypsy woman, likely the 'keep, as well.

'Wilkins!' yelled Jim, panic rising. 'Don't you hurt her. She doesn't know about the mine.'

Silence answered.

'Wilkins?' His shout rang in hollow echoes throughout the chamber, and no response came from the outside. With surging panic, Jim knew Wilkins was on his way to murder Grace.

* * *

When Grace entered the saloon the gypsy woman's gaze rose to meet hers and a flash of surprise crossed her features. It wasn't much of a stretch to figure out Grace had come here intending harm, not with the fury in her green eyes and the conviction in her stride. Guilt was suddenly plain on the olive-skinned woman's face, along with a measure of panic and Grace almost smiled. Catriona started to rise but Grace grabbed the gun from her holster and aimed it right between the woman's ample bosoms.

'What is the meaning of this?' The gypsy woman struggled to keep an indignant tone but failed. She eased herself back into the chair, keeping her hands on the table.

Grace thumbed back the hammer and stopped at the edge of the table. The gypsy woman's dark eyes lost most of their fear and reflected a look of utter viciousness.

'I want that title back.' Grace's voice came cold, with a tone that said she'd accept no argument.

'I do not understand. I have no title.' The gypsy woman's voice sounded too sincere and Grace knew she was lying.

'You best think that over, Madam Fortune-Teller, 'fore I just put lead twixt your eyes. You killed my uncle.'

Catriona seemed to contemplate the odds that Grace would pull the trigger and evidently decided they weren't in her favor. Her hand drifted to her bosom in a gesture that would only look natural on a flustered southern belle.

Grace's face pinched. 'I wouldn't try it if I were you. Ain't much holding me back from pulling this trigger as it is.' In truth, she wasn't sure she could kill the woman in cold blood. She had never been faced with actually going through with shooting a human being and she reckoned anger and grief were driving her now, not the killer instinct. Her hand began to quake as she held the gun straight-armed.

The 'keep stood frozen behind the bar. Grace could see him from the corner of her eye.

The gypsy woman lowered her hand, apparently thinking better of challenging Grace for the moment. 'Please, let us discuss this, Grace Crowly. I am sure everything can be worked out.'

Muscles knotted to either side of Grace's jaw; her fingers bleached as they squeezed the gun tighter. 'Ain't nothin' to work out. My uncle's dead and it's your fault, way I see it. You took his title. I want it back. Then you and me, we're gonna go see the marshal.'

'Marshal's a bit occupied, I'm afraid, my dear cousin.'

As the voice sounded from behind her, a chill slithered down her spine. She didn't have to turn to know Orville Wilkins was standing there, likely leveling a gun on her back. 'You best not have done anything to him, you sonofabitch.'

'I have done nothing to him, I assure you. Time will accomplish that for me. Now drop your gun or I'll put a bullet in your back.'

Grace considered whirling and trying to shoot it out with him. She was likely the better shot but he held a far greater advantage. The moment she made a wrong move she would be dead.

Her eyes locked with the gypsy's. Catriona had a widening smirk on her face. If what Orville intended to do to her person out in the woods was any indication, the dark-skinned woman was due to have that smug expression wiped clean off her face right soon. Grace lowered her arm, placing the gun on the table. 'Now back away, towards the bar,' Orville said.

She complied, turning, backing to the counter. The 'keep had started to shake and Catriona's hand was drifting towards her bosom again.

Orville walked deeper into the barroom, looking like a cat who had just swallowed a bird. The Smith & Wesson in his hand never wavered. He glanced at the barkeep. 'I don't need you . . . ' With shocking suddenness, he swung his aim to the saloon man and blasted a shot. Crimson exploded across the man's white shirt and shock froze on his features. He slammed back into a hutch filled with bottles, the bottles crashing to the floor with his body. Grace let out a gasp, horror filling her at the sheer brutal casualness of the act.

The smug expression dropped from Catriona's face, replaced by panic. Her hand shot to her bosom and she got a derringer out just as Orville swung the gun on her and fired.

'Don't need you, either . . . ' he said, as the woman flew backwards out of her chair and landed in a lifeless heap on the floor. Sawdust settled over her body.

Orville turned his attention back to Grace. 'I want the title to that mine, Grace, and I want it now.'

'You just killed your chances of gettin' it, you sonofabitch. The gypsy stole it.'

Orville studied her, apparently deciding she was telling the truth. 'Go search her body and be quick about it.'

Grace was less than thrilled with the prospect but saw little choice but to obey. She went to the dead gypsy and knelt, going through her skirt pockets. She pulled out a piece of folded paper and stood.

Orville let out a small laugh. 'Thank you kindly, Grace. You saved me a trip back to their camp to search for it.

However, it does present me with a bit of a quandary. You see, I wanted to show you just how wrong it was to treat me the way you did when we were young'uns, the way you treated me in the woods earlier today. But I reckon maybe you're just too troublesome to leave alive while I dispose of these bodies.'

She locked gazes with him and his eyes reflected her death. 'You're still a lowly sonofabitch. You'll never be nothing more.'

He smiled. 'I can live with that . . . set the title on the table. I don't want it full of blood.'

She hesitated, mind searching for a way out of the situation, a way she could get to him first and make him pay for everything he had done. He would kill her the moment she placed the title on the table. That left her with no choice but to try a desperate move. Before she could think on it, she flung the title at him, at the same time hurling herself sideways and making a grab for her gun on the table.

Orville must have anticipated the move because he lunged, covering the distance between them faster than she would have thought possible. By the time she reached her gun he was on her. He swung his own weapon at her chin. The butt connected with a resounding *clack* and she dropped, blood filling her mouth and senses spinning.

Orville's laugh thundered in her ears like a demon telling her he had just claimed her soul. He knelt and leaned over her, a sick grin on his face as he jammed the barrel against her forehead.

★   ★   ★

Wilkins was on his way to kill Grace and Jim Morgan could do nothing to stop him unless his theory about the gypsies having a secret way out of the saloon proved right. With a glance at the rocks blocking the entrance, he knew digging out was impossible; it would take months and time was an option he didn't have. His only chance was following the shaft.

He retrieved his gun, shoved it into its holster, then peered down the tunnel. Wavering lantern-light flickered in monstrous marbled shapes of amber and shadow on the walls. If the tunnel didn't lead to a way out, or branched off into numerous tributaries, he was a dead man.

'You best be right about this, Morgan . . . ' he whispered, starting forward. He grabbed the first lantern he came to and held it out before him. As he went on, the shaft began to slope gradually and that brought a measure of hope. If it led into town and under the saloon it would have to dip a good fifty feet.

Twenty feet later, the tunnel narrowed, walls sporting a more chiseled appearance. He noted hollows gouged deep into rock where he reckoned ore had been hacked out with a pick. Minerals embedded into the walls sparkled under the lantern-light and veins of quartz glittered.

The air thinned and his breathing grew shallow, labored. His legs were starting to turn rubbery and sweat streamed down his face and chest. A dull throbbing ache pulsated across the back of his skull from the explosion that sealed the mine entrance.

He judged he'd traversed at least a half-mile and that should have put him well into town. Before him, bluish veins widened, in some places spanning nearly twenty feet across. Pausing, he ran his fingers along the wall's surface. The deposit felt warm, gritty. The quartz surrounding it captured flame-light from his lantern and shimmered with a topaz glow.

While he knew damn little about silver-mining, it was enough to realize the old man's title had given him claim to riches beyond anything he or Grace imagined. It was likely the largest strike this side of Leadville. Bluish rivers of silver appeared endless, in places darkening in color, indicating the ore was laced with gold. Jim let out a low whistle, awestruck, but quickly shook off the feeling.

Moving forward again, he noticed the temperature rose by a good ten degrees, which was not uncommon in mines and likely the result of an underground reservoir somewhere deep below. He had heard tell of miners in Leadville hitting pockets of steam that spewed vapor superheated to 160 degrees. Many miners labored in their underwear.

Another hundred yards went by and he stopped. A number of mining tools — picks and shovels, a sledge-hammer and buckets — lay scattered along the tunnel floor. Mounds of ore lined the wall, bulging sacks stacked close by. Going to the sacks and kneeling, he discovered they were filled with pulverized ore, much of it fine enough to be sand. An assayer would likely have placed the value somewhere around $3,000 per ton in silver alone. Add to that the gold content and whoever owned the mine was looking at millions of dollars worth of potential yield.

Jim straightened, peering about the tunnel. To his left, about twenty feet on, was a makeshift ladder leading straight up into the shaft ceiling. He went to it, noting a number of hooks pounded into the wall to the right of the ladder. One of the hooks held a velvet robe. The gypsy woman changed down here after her mysterious exits; that's why her robe had picked up enough silver dust to leave a coating behind on her chair.

Setting the lantern on a hook, he gripped the edges of the ladder and started up. He wagered the prospector who discovered the mine and built Silver Bluff had also constructed the ladder because it was rickety as hell. The rungs groaned under each of his steps.

Half-way up, the shaft turned from rock to wooden walls, much like those of dumbwaiter shafts in some of the fancier houses he had seen in Austin. Reaching the top, he felt along the wall.

Locating a latch, he slid the bolt to the left. Hand flat on the surface, he applied pressure and a panel swung outward. Dim light flooded into the shaft. Crawling through the opening, he came out inside the saloon's storeroom. The panel, nearly seamless, was on the room's south wall behind a row of barrels. It was unlikely anyone would have spotted the exit unless specifically searching for it.

Any sense of relief at escaping and discovering the gypsies' secret was short-lived, because a blast sounded from beyond the storeroom door. He jolted. Panic made his heart stutter. That blast meant Wilkins had reached the saloon and had likely just murdered the gypsy woman or the barkeep.

Unless Grace hadn't stayed in her room the way you warned her to. .

A second blast sounded and he snatched his Colt from its holster. Hurtling across the room, he threw open the door and lunged into the hallway. He whipped to the door leading to the saloon proper, which gaped open. He paused, listening, but no further shots came.

Heart pounding in his throat, he eased aside the velvet curtain.

He damn near uttered a gasp of relief, though the scene that met him was one of carnage and danger. The gypsy woman lay sprawled just beyond his feet, dead. A few feet away, a man hovered over Grace, jamming a gun to her forehead. He had no doubt the man was Orville Wilkins and only seconds remained before a third shot sent the young woman's brains splattering across the sawdust.

Morgan's gun swept up, leveling on the man's chest. He hesitated, knowing he could kill Wilkins easily enough but reflex might cause the killer to pull his own trigger.

'Wilkins!' Jim yelled, seeing only one chance: distract the killer, get him to aim for another target. The man's head jerked up. Shock flashed across his face and he reacted the way Jim hoped.

Orville swung the gun towards the new threat. The speed at which the man's hand whisked around nearly caught Jim flat-footed and he might not have fired in time had Grace not suddenly jerked up her knee and buried it in Orville's middle.

A pained look flashed across Orville's face but his aim faltered only an instant.

That instant was enough.

Jim fired and lead punched into Wilkins's chest. Scarlet exploded in a starburst across the man's shirt. The impact kicked him backwards. He slammed into the floor, struggling to get up, making strangled sounds as blood bubbled from his lips. With a gasp and a spray of crimson from his lips, Wilkins fell back, spasmed, then voided in death.

Grace wasted no time leaping to her feet as Jim stepped over the gypsy's body. She fell into his arms and began to sob. He held her until dusk filled the saloon and the ghosts of the past haunted the El Silverado no more.

★ ★ ★

Gunmetal clouds blanketed the morning sky and dusky shadows swarmed over the small graveyard at the outskirts of Silver Bluff. Grace, wearing the blue dress Jim had bought for her, paused before a grave adorned with only a simple wooden marker that soon would be replaced with a stone. He stood just behind her, heart heavy and sorrow aching in his soul for a man he had met only a short time ago, but one who had touched his life in ways he would never have expected. If Phidias Crowly had never achieved anything he considered a success in life, he had certainly achieved it in death. He had left his niece a life of security and wealth, and gifted Jim Morgan with a treasure far beyond anything that could be measured in ingots of silver: a woman named Grace Crowly.

Head down, voice low and trembling, she said, 'He never got his dream . . .'

Jim frowned, twisting the brim of the

Stetson in his hands. 'He got it, Grace. He wanted you to be set for life, so you wouldn't always be searchin' for something in vain, the way he did. You won't want for nothin' ever again with that silver-mine to your name.'

She uttered a mocking laugh. 'You got that wrong, Marshal. What I want outa life ain't got much to do with silver-mines; it's got more to do with folks lost.'

He nodded, emotion choking his throat. He wished he could console her but damn little he could say would make a difference. He couldn't bring her uncle back; only time would ease the sting of her loss.

He set his hat on his head and headed towards the gate. He would let her be for now, let her say her goodbyes as she needed. He had no right to intrude on her tears.

'You just gonna walk away . . . ?'

Her voice stopped him at the gate and he turned to see a tear slipping down her face.

He shrugged. 'You askin' me to stay?'

She looked at the ground, a sob shuddering through her body. When she looked up, she mouthed the word yes and more tears wandered down her face.

His breath caught and he offered a weak smile. 'I had my choice I'd ask you to marry me. But I'm a small-town marshal and you're a rich woman now. You could do better.'

She uttered a fragile laugh. 'I reckon I couldn't, Marshal, and I can't run a silver-mine alone. I ain't the kind of gal most men would consider settlin' down with, and I know I spent too many years hiding my feelings but this time I aim to meet them head on. Those feelings are tellin' me I love you, Jim Morgan.'

'You ain't known me long, Grace. Might be a bumpy trail.'

She laughed and her tone carried a note of irony. 'Ain't it always?'

He smiled and went to her. With Grace Crowly at his side, he reckoned nothing in Silver Bluff would ever be mundane again.

We do hope that you have enjoyed reading this large print book.

Did you know that all of our titles are available for purchase?

We publish a wide range of high quality large print books including:
Romances, Mysteries, Classics
General Fiction
Non Fiction and Westerns

Special interest titles available in large print are:
The Little Oxford Dictionary
Music Book, Song Book
Hymn Book, Service Book

Also available from us courtesy of Oxford University Press:
Young Readers' Dictionary
(large print edition)
Young Readers' Thesaurus
(large print edition)

For further information or a free brochure, please contact us at:
Ulverscroft Large Print Books Ltd.,
The Green, Bradgate Road, Anstey,
Leicester, LE7 7FU, England.
Tel: (00 44) **0116 236 4325**
Fax: (00 44) **0116 234 0205**

THE WIND WAGON

Troy Howard

Sheriff Al Corning was as tough as they came and with his four seasoned deputies he kept the peace in Laramie — at least until the squatters came. To fend off starvation, the settlers took some cattle off the cowmen, including Jonas Lefler. A hard, unforgiving man, Lefler retaliated with lynchings. Things got worse when one of the squatters revealed he was a former Texas lawman — and no mean shooter. Could Sheriff Corning prevent further bloodshed?

CABEL

Paul K. McAfee

Josh Cabel returned home from the Civil War to find his family all murdered by rioting members of Quantrill's band. The hunt for the killers led Josh to Colorado City where, after months of searching, he finally settled down to work on a ranch nearby. He saved the life of an Indian, who led him to a cache of weapons waiting for Sitting Bull's attack on the Whites. His involvement threw Cabel into grave danger. When the final confrontation came, who had the fastest — and deadlier — draw?

When Rufus Blake died he was
found to be carrying a gold bar
from a Confederate gold shipment
that had disappeared twenty years
before. This inspires Wes Hardiman
and Ben Travis to swap horse and
trail for a riverboat, the *River
Queen*, on the Mississippi, in an
effort to find the missing gold. Cord
Duval is set on destroying the *River
Queen* and he has the power and the
gunmen to do it. Guns blaze as
Hardiman and Travis attempt to
unravel the mystery and stay alive.